# A sexy smile touched the corners of his lips.

"I've wanted to kiss you from the moment I saw you."

Bristol drew in a deep breath and stared at him. "I just can't believe you are alive. Someone in the State Department checked into it and told me you'd died."

"When was this?"

"A month after I last saw you."

He nodded. "I was presumed dead, so the person was right. I was rescued just days before Christmas the following year."

"That was a long time."

"Yes, it was." Only his close friends knew about the nightmares he'd had for months following his rescue. Nightmares he still had at times.

"Why were you trying to reach me, Bristol?"

Drawing in another deep breath, she met his gaze and said, "I wanted to let you know I was pregnant."

\* \* \*

*His Secret Son* is part of
The Westmoreland Legacy—

Friends and relatives of the legendary
Westmoreland family find love!

Dear Reader,

I love writing about families, and the Westmorelands continue to be one of my favorites. In the beginning, there were so many Westmorelands, I figured they could befriend themselves and I didn't need to introduce any close friends. But then I gave Derringer a best friend with Grant "Pete" Higgins. After that, I decided when I wrote Bane's story I would give him close friends, as well. Friends who were fellow SEALs—Viper, Coop, Flipper and Mac. These were Bane's friends I wanted to know better.

You met Viper in *The Rancher Returns* and now I want to introduce you to Laramie "Coop" Cooper. There was so much about Coop I wanted to know. I enjoyed writing his story and placing him in the life of Bristol Lockett. And more than anything, I wanted Coop to get to know the son he hadn't known he had.

Look for Flipper's story in 2018!

Thank you for wanting to know the Westmorelands' friends. I look forward to bringing you more books of endless love and red-hot passion.

Happy Reading!

*Brenda Jackson*

# BRENDA JACKSON

## HIS SECRET SON

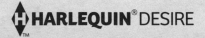

Recycling programs
for this product may
not exist in your area.

ISBN-13: 978-0-373-83884-4

His Secret Son

Copyright © 2017 by Brenda Streater Jackson

All rights reserved. Except for use in any review, the reproduction or utilization of this work in whole or in part in any form by any electronic, mechanical or other means, now known or hereinafter invented, including xerography, photocopying and recording, or in any information storage or retrieval system, is forbidden without the written permission of the publisher, Harlequin Enterprises Limited, 225 Duncan Mill Road, Don Mills, Ontario M3B 3K9, Canada.

This is a work of fiction. Names, characters, places and incidents are either the product of the author's imagination or are used fictitiously, and any resemblance to actual persons, living or dead, business establishments, events or locales is entirely coincidental.

This edition published by arrangement with Harlequin Books S.A.

For questions and comments about the quality of this book, please contact us at CustomerService@Harlequin.com.

® and TM are trademarks of Harlequin Enterprises Limited or its corporate affiliates. Trademarks indicated with ® are registered in the United States Patent and Trademark Office, the Canadian Intellectual Property Office and in other countries.

Printed in U.S.A.

**Brenda Jackson** is a *New York Times* bestselling author of more than one hundred romance titles. Brenda lives in Jacksonville, Florida, and divides her time between family, writing and traveling.

Email Brenda at authorbrendajackson@gmail.com or visit her on her website at brendajackson.net.

### Books by Brenda Jackson

### Harlequin Desire

#### The Westmorelands

*A Wife for a Westmoreland*
*The Proposal*
*Feeling the Heat*
*Texas Wild*
*One Winter's Night*
*Zane*
*Canyon*
*Stern*
*The Real Thing*
*The Secret Affair*
*Breaking Bailey's Rules*
*Bane*

#### The Westmoreland Legacy

*The Rancher Returns*
*His Secret Son*

Visit her Author Profile page at Harlequin.com, or brendajackson.net, for more titles!

To the man who will always and forever
have my heart, Gerald Jackson Sr.

To Cozett Mazelin and Tamira K. Butler-Likely.
Thanks for your assistance in my research of
two-year-olds. Your information was invaluable
and I hope I did the character of "Little Laramie"
justice! I could tell from your responses
that you are great moms!!

To my readers who continue to love my
Westmorelands, this book is for you.

For none of us lives for ourselves alone,
and none of us dies for ourselves alone.

—*Romans* 14:7, NIV

# Prologue

Bristol Lockett hurriedly moved toward her front door, wondering who would be visiting this late in the afternoon. Although it was still light outside, this particular Paris community was on the other side of town from the famous city center, where most people hung out on Friday nights and weekends. Normally, she would be there herself, but her habits had changed in the last couple of months.

She was one of those pregnant women who experienced morning sickness in the morning and at night. Smells alone would send her running to the nearest bathroom. Most morning sickness lasted until the twelfth week of pregnancy. She was in her sixteenth week and there didn't seem to be an end in sight. Her doctor had even placed her on a special diet to make sure she was getting sufficient nutrients into her body for her baby.

A glance out the peephole indicated her visitor was her best friend, Dionne Burcet. She and Dionne had met when Bristol first arrived in Paris four years ago to attend Académie des Beaux-Arts, which was considered one of the most prestigious and influential art schools in all of France. Dionne also attended the art academy and with so much in common, they'd hit it off immediately.

Dionne, who'd been born in Paris, had introduced Bristol to French culture, and Bristol had taken Dionne home with her to America last Christmas to meet her aunt Dolly and to experience New Year's Eve in New York. A feeling of sadness fell over Bristol whenever she remembered that was the last holiday she and her aunt had spent together. Her aunt, her only relative, had died a few days later in her sleep.

Bristol opened the door smiling. "Dionne! This is a surprise. I thought you were leaving for—"

"I have something to tell you, Bristol."

Bristol heard the urgency in Dionne's voice, which resonated in her eyes, as well. "Okay, come on in. Would you like a cup of tea? I was just about to make a pot."

"Yes, thanks."

Bristol wondered about Dionne's strange demeanor as she led her friend to the kitchen, which wasn't far from the front door. She loved her studio apartment. It was small but just the right size for her. And it held a lot of memories. Her baby was conceived here, in her bed. She would miss this place when she moved back to the United States next month after graduation.

"Sit and tell me what's wrong. Did you and Mark have a fight?"

Dionne shook her head as she sat down at the table. "No. It's not about me, it's about you."

"Me?" Bristol said in surprise.

"Yes. You remember what you shared with me last month?"

"Yes. I told you I was pregnant." Telling Dionne hadn't been easy but she'd felt the need to confide in someone. The baby's father was a man she'd met one day at a café. He had been a US navy SEAL out with a few of his friends and he'd flirted with her outrageously. She'd done something she had never done before and flirted back. There had been something about Laramie Cooper that had made her behave like a different person and for the next three days, over the Christmas holidays, they had enjoyed a holiday fling. It was a period in her life she would never forget. Her pregnancy made certain of that.

"Yes, from that guy. The American soldier."

"Not just a soldier, Dionne. Laramie was a navy SEAL," Bristol said, smiling proudly.

"Yes, the navy SEAL Laramie Cooper," Dionne said.

From the time they'd been introduced, Bristol had liked his name and he'd said he liked hers. Laramie had told her very little about his work or even about himself. She knew he was an only child and his parents were still living in the US. He hadn't said where.

Bristol regretted that Dionne had been away visiting her grandparents in Marseille for the holidays and hadn't been around to meet Laramie. She believed her friend would have liked him. "What about him?"

"You told me how the two of you spent time together over the holidays and since finding out you were pregnant, you've been trying to locate him to let him know."

Since she'd known very little about Laramie, other than his name and age, she had mailed a letter to him in care of the US Navy. The letter had been returned weeks ago stamped UNABLE TO LOCATE.

"Yes, and like I told you, it doesn't matter to me that our time together was a no-strings affair, I believe he has a right to know about his child. I refused to do to him what my mother did to my father."

For years, Bristol never knew her father and, according to her mother, she never told her father about Bristol. It was information her mother had taken with her to the grave. It was only after her mother's death that Bristol's aunt Dolly had given her the man's name. She had met Randall Lockett at sixteen. He had been surprised to find out about her and had welcomed her into his life.

"Yes, I know. That's why I decided to help you."

Bristol raised a brow. "Help me?"

"Yes."

"How?"

"Remember I told you about that guy—an American—I dated years ago? The one who worked at your embassy?"

"Yes, I remember."

"Well, he was recently reassigned back to the embassy here and I ran into him. I gave him your SEAL's name and asked if he would try locating him and forwarding him a message to contact you."

Happiness eased into Bristol and spread to all parts

of her body. Although it might have been nothing more than a holiday fling for Laramie Cooper, it had been a lot more for her. She had fallen in love with him. "Was your friend able to find him?"

Dionne slowly nodded her head. "Yes."

Bristol stared at her friend, knowing there was more. The happiness she felt earlier began dissipating at the sadness she saw in Dionne's eyes. "What is it, Dionne? What did you find out?"

All sorts of things began rushing through her mind. What if Laramie hadn't been the single man he'd claimed to be and had a wife and children somewhere? When Dionne didn't say anything, but looked down at the cup of tea Bristol had placed in front of her, Bristol slouched her shoulders in disappointment. "I think I know why you're hesitating in telling me."

Dionne looked back at her. "Do you?"

"Yes. He's married. Although he told me he wasn't, you found out differently, didn't you?"

"Bristol."

"It doesn't matter. He has a right to know about his child anyway. If he decides never to be a part of my baby's life, it will be his decision and—"

"That's not it, Bristol," Dionne cut in to say.

Bristol frowned. "Then what is it?"

Dionne took a sip of her tea, hesitating. The dawdling was driving Bristol crazy. "For Pete's sake, Dionne, will you just get it out and tell me what you found out about Laramie?"

Dionne held her gaze and drew in a deep breath. "Some mission he was on went bad and he was killed. He's dead, Bristol."

# One

*The Naval Amphibious Base Coronado, San Diego, California, three years later*

"Let me get this straight, Lieutenant Cooper. You actually want to give up your holiday leave and remain here and work on base?"

Laramie "Coop" Cooper forced his smile to stay in place while answering his commanding officer's question. "Yes, sir. I actually want to do that."

He wouldn't tell anyone that he'd looked forward to going home for the holidays, because honestly, he hadn't. The phone call he'd gotten from his parents that they would be jet-setting to London again this year was expected. They'd done so every holiday for as long as he could remember. He doubted they'd even canceled those plans that Christmas three years ago when they'd thought him dead.

At thirty-two, he had stopped letting his parents' actions affect him. As far as Ryan and Cassandra Cooper were concerned, the universe revolved around them and nobody else. Especially not a son who, at times, they seemed to forget existed. It wasn't that he thought his parents didn't love him; he knew they did. They just loved each other more. He had long ago accepted that his parents believed there were different degrees of love, and that the love they shared for each other outweighed the love for their child.

In a way, he should be glad that after thirty-five years of marriage his parents were still that into each other. They shared something special, had this unbreakable bond, and some would even say it was the love of a lifetime. But on the other hand, that love never extended to him in the same degree. He knew their lack of affection had nothing to do with his deciding to become a navy SEAL instead of joining his parents' multimillion-dollar manufacturing company. His father had understood Laramie's desire to make his decisions based on what he wanted to do with his life, and he appreciated his dad for accepting that.

More holidays than not, for as far back as Laramie could remember, he'd been packed up and shipped off to his paternal grandparents' ranch in Laredo. Not that he was complaining. His grandparents had been the best and hadn't hesitated to show him the degree of love he'd lacked at home. In fact, he would admit to resenting his parents when they did show up at his grandparents' ranch to get him.

So, here he was volunteering to give up his holiday

leave. It wasn't as if he hadn't received invitations from his SEAL teammates to join them and their families for the holidays, because he had. Bane Westmoreland— code name Bane—had been the first to invite Laramie to spend the holidays with his family in Denver. But given the fact that Bane's wife, Crystal, had given birth to triplets six months ago, Laramie didn't want to get underfoot.

Same thing with Thurston McRoy—code name Mac—with his wife, Teri, and their four kids. Gavin Blake—code name Viper—would be celebrating his first Christmas as a married man so Laramie didn't want to intrude there, either. The only other single guy in the group was David Holloway—code name Flipper. Flipper came from a huge family of four brothers, who were all SEALs, and a father who'd retired as a SEAL commanding officer. Laramie had spent the holidays with Flipper's family last year and didn't want to wear out his welcome.

"I'm denying your request, Lieutenant."

His commanding officer's words recaptured Laramie's attention. He met the man's gaze and tried to keep a frown off his face. "May I ask why, sir?"

"I think you know the reason. SEAL Team Six, of which you are a vital member, has been pretty damn busy this year. I don't have to list all the covert operations successfully accomplished with very few casualties. You deserve your holiday leave."

"Even if I don't want to take it?"

His commanding officer held his gaze. "Yes, even if you don't want to take it. Military leave is necessary, especially for a SEAL, to recoup both mentally and physically. Don't think I haven't noticed how much you've been pushing yourself. It's like you're trying to make up for the time you were a captive in Syria."

Laramie remembered all eleven months of being held prisoner in that guerilla hellhole. He hadn't known from one day to the next if he'd survive that day. The bastards had done everything in their power to make him think every day would be his last. They'd even played Russian roulette with him a couple of times.

It was on one of those particular days when he'd been rescued. Leave it to Bane, who was a master sniper, to bring down the four men from a distance of over a hundred feet. Laramie was convinced there was no way he would have survived if his SEAL team hadn't shown up.

During those eleven months he'd fought hard to stay sane and the one memory that had sustained him was the face of the woman he'd met in Paris just weeks before the mission.

Bristol Lockett.

It had been a three-day holiday affair. Sadly, there was little he knew about her other than sharing her bed had been the best sexual experience of his life.

"However, since I know you're going to insist," his commanding officer said, reclaiming Laramie's thoughts again, "I've got an important job that I want you to do. However, it means traveling to New York."

Laramie raised a brow. "New York?"

"Yes. An important delivery needs to be made to a member of the United Nations Security Council."

Laramie wondered what kind of delivery. Classified documents no doubt.

He'd heard how beautiful Manhattan was when it

was decorated for this time of year. He'd been to the Big Apple a number of times, but never around the holidays. "Once I make the delivery, sir. Then what?"

"That, Lieutenant, is up to you. If you decide to take your holiday leave, then you won't have to report back here until the end of January as scheduled. However, if you still want to give up your leave, then you're free to come back here and I'll find more work for you to do."

Laramie nodded. He might take a week off to enjoy the sights and sounds of New York, but there was no doubt in his mind that he would be returning to San Diego for more work.

Bristol glanced around the art gallery. She always felt a sense of pride and accomplishment whenever she saw one of her paintings on display. Especially here at the Jazlyn Art Gallery of New York. She wanted to pinch herself to make sure she wasn't dreaming.

She had worked so hard for this moment.

"Looks good, doesn't it?"

She glanced up at her manager, Margie Townsend. "Yes, I have to admit that it does."

Margie's tenacious pit bull–like skills had landed Bristol a showing at this gallery, one of the most well-known and highly respected galleries in New York. She and Margie had met last year on the subway and struck up a conversation. When Bristol discovered what Margie did for a living, she felt their chance encounter must have been an omen. She'd invited Margie to her home to see her work, and the excitement reflected in the woman's eyes had been incredible. Margie promised to change Bristol's life. She promised that Bristol would get to the point where she could quit her job as an assistant magazine editor and make her living as the artist she was born to be.

Less than eight months later, Margie had sold one of Bristol's paintings. The buyer had been so taken with her work that he'd also purchased several others. The money had been enough to bring about the change in Bristol's life Margie had guaranteed. She had turned in her resignation and now painted full-time in her home.

Bristol was happy with the direction of her career. She got to spend more time with her son since she kept him with her every day instead of taking him to day care like she used to do.

Her son.

She smiled when she thought about her rambunctious two-year old—the most important person in her life. He was her life. Every decision she made was done with him in mind. She'd already started a college fund for him and couldn't wait to share the holidays with him. Last night they had put up their Christmas tree. Correction, she thought, widening her smile. She had put up the tree. Laramie had gotten in the way with his anxiousness to help.

Laramie…

It was hard not to think of Laramie's father whenever she thought of her son. She had named him after his biological father, Laramie Cooper, who had died way too young, and without knowing about the child they'd created together. Sometimes she wondered what he would have done had he lived and gotten the letter she'd tried to send him.

Would he have been just as happy as she'd been? Or would he have claimed the child wasn't his? She might not have known Laramie Cooper long, but she wanted to believe he was a man who would have wanted to be a part of his child's life. The way her father had wanted to be a part of hers. The two years she'd shared with the man who'd fathered her had not been enough.

"Are you ready to go? You have a big day tomorrow and I want you well rested."

She chuckled as she tightened her coat around her. "And I will be."

Margie rolled her eyes. "I guess as much as you can be with a two-year-old running around the place."

She knew what Margie was hinting at. Bristol was spending less and less time painting now that Laramie was in the terrible twos. It was also the get-into-everything twos. The only time she really got to paint was during his nap time or while he slept at night.

"Did you give any more thought to what I said?"

Margie had suggested that she send Laramie to day care two to three days a week. "Yes, but I'm thinking of hiring someone to come to my home instead of me having to take him somewhere."

"That might work, but he has to start learning to interact with other kids, Bristol." As they walked toward the waiting private car that was compliments of the gallery, Margie changed the subject. "Have you decided to go out with Steven?"

Bristol shrugged. Steven Culpepper was nice enough, and good-looking, too. However, he was moving too fast. At least, faster than she liked. They'd met a few weeks ago when she'd closed a huge deal for a commissioned piece. He was the corporation's attorney. He'd asked for her number and, without thinking much about it, she'd given it to him. Since then he'd called constantly, trying to get her to go out with him. So far, she hadn't. She hated pushy men and Steven, she thought, was one of the pushiest.

"No."

"I like him."

Bristol grinned. "You would. You have a thing for wealthy businessmen." She knew Margie had been married to one. Or two. She was on her third marriage and not even fifty yet. But the one thing all three men had in common was the size of their bank accounts.

"Well, I know you still have a thing for Laramie's father and—"

"What makes you think that?"

"Bristol, you make it quite obvious that you haven't gotten over him."

Did she? The only thing she'd told Margie about Laramie's father was that he'd been in the military and had died in the line of duty without knowing he'd fathered a son. She'd even fabricated a tale that Laramie had been her deceased husband and not just her lover.

It had been pretty easy. Dionne's fiancé, Mark, had helped. Mark worked for a judge in Paris and had falsified the papers before Bristol left France. It was a way to make sure her son had his father's last name without people wondering why her last name was different. It wasn't as if she was trying to cash in on her son's father's military benefits or anything.

"If you ask me, I think you should finally move on…with Steven," Margie said, interrupting Bristol's thoughts.

Bristol wanted to say that nobody had asked Margie. But deep down, a part of her knew Margie was right. It was time for Bristol to move on. However, she doubted very seriously that it would be with Steven.

A short while later she was entering her home, a beautiful brownstone in Brooklyn that she'd inherited from her aunt Dolly. She loved the place and knew the neighborhood well. She'd come to live here with her aunt ten years ago, when she was fifteen. That had been the year her mother died.

She didn't want to think sad thoughts, especially after her positive meeting with Maurice Jazlyn, the owner of the gallery. The man was excited about tomorrow night's showing and expected a huge crowd. He loved all the artworks she would be exhibiting.

"How did things go tonight?"

She turned toward the older woman coming down the stairs to the main floor. Charlotte Kramer lived next door and had been a close friend of her aunt Dolly. With her four kids grown and living in other parts of New York, Ms. Charlotte had thought about moving to a condo not far away, but had decided she'd rather stay put since she'd lived in the area close to forty years and loved her neighbors. Ms. Charlotte said there were a lot of memories of Mr. Kramer stored in that house. He'd passed away eight years ago, a couple of years after Bristol had come to live with her aunt.

Bristol appreciated that Ms. Charlotte loved watching Laramie for her whenever she had meetings to attend. And Ms. Charlotte had offered to watch him again tomorrow night when Bristol attended the exhibition.

"Everything went well. Everyone is excited about tomorrow. Mr. Jazlyn thinks he'll be able to sell all my paintings."

A huge smile touched Ms. Charlotte's lips. "That's good news. Dolly would be proud. Candace would be, too."

She doubted the latter. Her mother had never approved of Bristol becoming an artist. It was only after she died that Bristol learned why. Her father had been an artist who'd broken things off with her mother to study in Paris. It was only after he'd left the country that her mother discovered her pregnancy. She'd known how to reach him but refused to let him know about his child. She had resented him for ending things with her to pursue his dream.

Bristol had been sixteen when she'd met her father for the first time. She would not have met him then if it hadn't been for her aunt's decision to break the promise she'd made to Bristol's mother years ago. Aunt Dolly wanted Bristol to know her father and vice versa. When Bristol was given the man's name, she had been shocked to find that the person whose art she'd admired for years was really her father.

She'd finally gotten the courage to contact him on her sixteenth birthday. Randall Lockett was married with a family when they'd finally met. He had two young sons—ages ten and twelve—with his wife Krista. Bristol was his only daughter and she favored him so much it was uncanny. She was also his only offspring who'd inherited his artistic gift.

When he'd died, he had bequeathed to her full tuition to the school he himself had attended in Paris as well as the vast majority of his paintings. He'd felt she would appreciate them more than anyone, and she had. She'd heard that Krista had remarried and sold off all the artworks that had been left to her and their sons.

Paintings by Randall Lockett were valued in the millions. Art collectors had contacted Bristol on numerous occasions, but she had refused to sell. Instead her father's paintings were on display at the two largest art museums in the world, New York's Metropolitan Museum of Art and the Orsay Museum in Paris.

A few months before her father had died, they had completed a painting together, which was her most cherished possession. It was so uncanny that when it came to art she and her father had possessed identical preferences. They even held their brushes the same way. On those days when she felt down and out, she would look at the portrait over her fireplace and remember the six weeks they'd spent together on his boat while painting it. That was when they'd noticed all the similarities they shared as artists. She hadn't known he was dying of cancer until his final days. He hadn't wanted her to know. He was determined to share every moment he could with her without seeing pity and regret in her eyes.

Forcing those sad thoughts from her mind, she glanced back over at Ms. Charlotte. "Did Laramie behave himself tonight?" she asked, placing her purse on the table.

The older woman chuckled. "Doesn't he always?"

Bristol smiled. "No, but I know you wouldn't tell me even if he was a handful."

"You're right, I wouldn't. Boys will be boys. I know. I raised four of them."

Yes, she had, and to this day Ms. Charlotte's sons looked out for her, making sure she had everything she needed and then some.

After Ms. Charlotte left, Bristol climbed the stairs

to her son's room. He was in his bed, sound asleep.
Crossing the bedroom floor, she saw he had put away
all his toys. That was a good sign that he was learning
to follow instructions.

Approaching the bed, she sat on the edge and gently ran her fingers through the curls on his head. He
favored his father. Laramie Cooper's features were
etched in her memory. Whenever Laramie smiled, he
displayed his father's dimples in both cheeks. Then
there was the shape of his mouth and the slant of his
eyes. Like father, like son. There was no doubt in her
mind that one day Laramie would grow up and cap-
ture some woman's heart just as quickly and easily as
his father had claimed hers.

As she sat there watching her son sleep, she couldn't
stop her mind from going back to that time in Paris
when she'd met US Navy SEAL Laramie Cooper…

# Two

Bristol glanced up from her sketch pad when she heard the male voices entering the café. Military men. All five of them. That was easy to deduce, even though they weren't wearing military attire. They were wearing jeans, shirts and dark leather jackets. The five walked confidently and were in perfect physical condition. Boy, were they ever! She wondered what branch of service they represented. It really didn't matter. Whichever one branch it was, they were representing it well.

The group took the table not far away from where she sat and one of the men, as if he felt someone staring at him, glanced over at her. Bam! She'd been caught. She hadn't averted her gaze back to her sketch pad quickly enough. For some reason, she knew without glancing back up that he was still looking at her. She could feel his gaze, just as if it was a physical caress. It made her heart beat faster. It seemed that every single hormone in her body had begun to sizzle. Nothing like that had ever happened to her before.

Okay, Bristol, concentrate on your sketch, she inwardly admonished herself. Her father hadn't paid her tuition at one of the most prestigious art schools in France for her to get all hot and bothered by a bunch of military men. Although the five were extremely handsome, it was only one of the men who had caught her eye. The one who'd stared back at her.

"Excuse me, miss."

She glanced up and the man was now standing at her table. Up close he was even more gorgeous. Definitely eye candy of the most delectable kind. Hot. Sexy. You name it and this man could definitely claim it. That had to be the reason intense heat was plowing up her spine.

Bristol swallowed deeply before saying, "Yes?"

"I was wondering if…"

When he didn't finish but kept looking at her, she asked. "Wondering what?"

"If I could join you?"

She wished he could but unfortunately, he couldn't. She glanced at her watch then back at him. "Sorry, but I work here and happen to be on my lunch break, which will end in less than five minutes."

"What time do you get off today?"

She tilted her head to look at him. "Excuse me?"

"I asked what time you get off today. I'll wait."

She figured that he had to be kidding, but the look

in his eyes showed that he wasn't. "I get off in four hours."

"I'll wait. What's your name?"

This guy was definitely moving fast. But she couldn't ignore the scorching hot attraction between them, even if she wanted to. And for some reason, she didn't want to. She liked it.

"My name is Bristol Lockett."

"The name Bristol is unusual. It suits you well. I like it."

And she liked his voice. It was deep and husky. The sound made heat curl inside her. OMG! What on earth was wrong with her? She'd never thought such outlandish things in her life. She might not have always been prim and proper but she'd been pretty close to it. She'd been in Paris close to four years and although she'd dated, most of the time she did not. She preferred curling up with her sketch pad and working on her watercolors than going out with any man. But now this ultrafine specimen was making her rethink that decision.

"Are you American or French?"

She blinked at his question. "I'm American."

"So am I."

She smiled. And what a good-looking American he was, with a body to die for. She felt as if she could draw her last breath just from looking at him. This guy was tall, at least six foot two or three. And his skin was the color of lightly roasted almonds. His dark eyes appeared somewhat slanted, and as far as she was concerned his lips were perfectly shaped. His hair was cut low on his head and his ears were just the right size for his face. But what captured her attention more than anything were those dimples in his cheeks. Doing absolutely nothing but standing there, he was arousing something within her that no other man ever had.

"And who are you?" she asked, deciding not to let him ask all the questions.

"I'm Laramie," he said, stretching out his hand to her.

She took it and immediately a spike of heat seemed to burst from his fingers and hit her dead center between the thighs. And when she stared into his eyes and saw the dark heat in his pupils, she knew he'd felt something, as well.

"Are you married, Laramie?"

"No. I've never been married. What about you? I approached you because I didn't see a ring on your finger."

At least he didn't hit on married women. Some men didn't care. "No, I'm not married, either, and never have been."

"So, Bristol Lockett, do I have your permission?"

She licked her lips. "For what?"

That sexy smile widened. "To be here when you get off."

Then what? she wondered but decided not to ask. "Sure, if that's what you want."

His chuckle made desire claw at her but it was his next words that sealed her fate. "There are a lot of things I want when it comes to you, Bristol."

Jeez. If he wasn't standing there she would close her eyes and moan. This man presented a temptation she shouldn't even think about yielding to. Too bad her best friend, Dionne, was out of town for the holidays and not around to talk some sense into her.

"What about if we share a drink at one of the pubs first?" she asked, and then frowned. Why had she made it sound as if she would be willing to move to the next stage once they shared a drink?

"That's fine. I'll be back in four hours."

When he walked off she glanced at her watch. Her break was officially over but she knew her encounter with this military man was just beginning.

She hurried behind the counter to put on her apron while watching Mary-Ann, another waitress, head over to the table to serve the five guys. More people entered the café, and Bristol was about to cross the room to serve a couple with a little girl when Mary-Ann stopped her.

"They asked for you," Mary-Ann said, smiling.

"Who?"

"Those soldiers. I've given them menus but they want you to serve their table. That's fine with me. Then I don't have to commit a sin by forgetting I've been married to Joel almost twenty years. Those five are too much temptation," she said, fanning herself. "I hope you can handle it."

Bristol hoped she could handle it as well, as she made her way to the table where all five men sat. Hot and heavy testosterone was thick in the air surrounding them. Drawing in a deep breath she approached them with her notepad in hand. "Have you guys decided what you're having?"

"Apparently, Coop has," one of the men said, grinning at her. "We're still deciding."

She nodded. "Okay, and who is Coop?"

"I am," the guy who had introduced himself to her earlier said.

She met his gaze. "I thought your name was Laramie."

He smiled again and she tried not to feel weak in the knees. "It is. My real name is Laramie Cooper. They call me Coop."

"Oh."

"Let me introduce everyone," Laramie said. "First off, guys, this is Bristol," he said to his friends.

"Hello, Bristol," they all said simultaneously as they stood to their feet, showing they had manners.

"Hello."

"I'm Bane," one of the men said, extending his hand to her.

She smiled at the very handsome military man as she shook his hand. "Hi, Bane."

"Is that a New York accent?" Bane asked.

"Yes, you would think after being in France for almost four years it would not be so easily detected."

Bane's smile widened. "Some things you can't get rid of."

"Apparently," she said, chuckling.

"I'm Flipper," another one of the guys said, offering his hand. He was definitely a hottie, with blond hair and the bluest eyes she'd ever seen. The color reminded her of the ocean and she wondered if that was why his nickname was Flipper.

"Nice meeting you, Flipper," she said, shaking his hand, as well.

"Same here, Bristol."

"I'm Mac," another one of the men said, leaning

across to take her hand. This man appeared older than the others by at least three or four years.

"Hi, Mac."

"And I'm Viper."

She glanced at the man who introduced himself as Viper. He was taller than the others and just as handsome. His eyes seemed sharp and penetrating. "Hi, Viper," she said, shaking his hand.

"Hi, Bristol," Viper returned, smiling.

"And you know me," Laramie said, taking her hand.

And just like before, a spike of heat hit her. "Yes, I know you." She quickly pulled her hand away. "It's nice meeting all of you and I like all your nicknames," she said as the men all sat back down.

Bane chuckled. "They aren't nicknames. They're our military code names."

"Oh. And what branch of the military?"

"We're navy SEALs," the one named Flipper said, grinning proudly.

He had every right to feel that way. She'd heard about navy SEALs. Some considered them the American government's secret weapon against any enemy force.

"So, Laramie, I'll start with you. What will you have?" she asked, getting ready to write on her notepad.

"For now I'll take a juicy hamburger, a large order of French fries and a huge malted strawberry shake."

For now? She wondered what he planned to have later. From the way he was looking at her, she had an idea. And why didn't realizing this guy evidently thought she was on his menu bother her?

Bristol went around the table and took everyone's

order. Apparently all five were big eaters and she wondered where they would put all that food and how they stayed in such great physical shape. After turning their orders in to the cook, she began waiting on other tables, but felt the heat of Laramie's gaze on her the entire time. Every time she glanced over in his direction, he was staring at her. Blatantly so.

Maybe it hadn't been a good idea for her to agree to have a drink with him when she got off work. She knew nothing about him, other than his name was Laramie Cooper, his military code name was Coop, he loved juicy hamburgers and he was a navy SEAL.

She delivered their food a short while later and watched them eat all of it. She could tell that the five were more than just members of the same military team. They shared a close friendship. That much was obvious from the way they joked around with each other.

Mac was married and had no problem showing her pictures of his wife and kids. It was evident he was proud of them. Bane, she'd discovered, was also married, but from the way the others teased him she could only assume he hadn't seen his wife in a while, which meant the two were separated. Like Laramie, Viper and Flipper were single and from the sound of things they intended to stay that way.

At the end of the meal when they paid their bill, she was shocked at the tip they left her. She would not normally have earned that much tip money in a week. "Thanks, guys."

"No, we want to thank you," Flipper said standing, like the others. "It was nice meeting you, Bristol, and the food was great."

The others shared the same sentiments as they moved to leave the café. Laramie hung back. "I'll be here when you get off work."

She knew now was a good time to tell him that she'd changed her mind about that. However, there was something about Laramie Cooper that made her hold back from doing so. It might have been his smile, or the way he was making her feel, or just the fact that she deserved to have some fun for a change.

For four years she had worked hard at the art academy and come spring she would be graduating. The café would be closing for the holidays and she had the next ten days off work. As far as she was concerned, there was nothing wrong with Laramie being there when she got off. They would just grab drinks at one of the pubs nearby. Besides, after today, she probably wouldn't see him again.

"I'll be waiting," she heard herself say.

She didn't have to wait. Laramie arrived a half hour before she was due to leave work. He ordered a croissant and coffee while he waited for her. She hung up her apron, wished everyone a Merry Christmas and then headed toward the table where he sat. He stood, smiling down at her.

"Ready?" he asked her.

"Yes" was her reply, although she wasn't sure what he had in mind and if she should be ready or not.

He surprised her by taking her hand, as if they both needed to feel the sexual chemistry between them. He led her through the doors and onto the sidewalk. Holiday decorations were everywhere. It was hard to believe tomorrow was Christmas Eve. Last year she had gone home for Christmas and had taken her best friend, Dionne, with her. But not this year. Her aunt Dolly had died in her sleep four days into the New Year.

She needed to stop thinking that she didn't have any living relatives when she had two brothers and a stepmother. She knew they'd only tolerated her while her father was alive and now, with him gone, they had let her know—by not returning her calls or letters—that they didn't have to put up with her anymore. That was fine. She'd adjusted to being a loner. At least she had Dionne and Dionne's family. The thought had even crossed Bristol's mind that she should not return to the United States after graduation and make Paris her home.

"Which pub are we going to?" she asked the man who was walking beside her and still holding her hand.

He smiled down at her. "Which one do you suggest?"

"Charlie's is a good one. It's right around the corner."

They didn't say much as they walked to the pub. They talked about the holidays. He told her that he and his team would be headed out in four days and they were in Paris for a little R and R.

"Your friends are nice," she said.

He smiled down at her as they continued walking. "They said the same thing about you."

She smiled at that, while trying to ignore all that desire she saw in his eyes. She figured if they kept talking it would go away. "The five of you seem close."

"We are. In fact, we're like brothers. Viper, Flipper, Bane and I attended the naval academy together and immediately became the best of friends. Mac is

four years older and finished the academy ahead of
us. He's been a SEAL longer and likes to think he's
looking out for us."

They reached the pub and saw it was crowded with
no tables available. It seemed everyone had decided to
begin celebrating the holidays early. "I have an idea,"
Laramie said, tightening his hand on hers.

"What?"

"Let's go someplace private."

An uneasy feeling crept over her, but it was over-
powered by exciting sensations that settled in her
stomach. Their hands were still joined and his fingers felt warm and reassuring.

"I want to be honest with you about something."

She swallowed. "About what?"

"Usually I spend the holidays alone, but I want to
spend them with you."

She held his gaze a minute and then asked, "What
about your friends?"

"They'll be in touch with their families."

"But you won't?"

He didn't say anything for a moment and then he
said, "My parents are still alive. I'm their only child.
But we've never spent the holidays together."

She found that odd. Christmas was the one holiday
she never had to worry about being alone. Her mother
had always made it special and after her mother's death,
her aunt Dolly had been there for her. She'd even spent
one Christmas with her father. It had been the first
and last holiday they'd spent together. This would be
the first Christmas that she had no one. She thought it
sad that Laramie had never really spent his holidays
with family.

She saw the sincerity in his eyes, in what he'd told her. He wasn't trying to feed her a pity line but was telling her the truth. She felt it in her heart.

"I can think of a place we can go," she suggested.

"Where?"

She knew it would be crazy to invite him, a perfect stranger to her home, but she was about to issue the invitation. "My place. It's not far from here. Just so happens I was going to be alone for the holidays as well and would love some company."

His hand tightened on hers. "You sure?"

Was she? She had never done anything so daring in her life.

She wasn't a child. She knew the obvious signs. Desire was thick between them. Spontaneous combustion as volatile as it could get. She dated infrequently and most guys who'd hit on her had tried to work her. But she would say that Laramie was the first guy who'd tried and managed to elicit her interest. He was also the first guy she was trusting to this degree. She had never invited a man to her home before. There had to be a reason for her doing so now.

"Yes. I'm sure," she said.

From the way his lips spread into a smile, she knew her response had pleased him. "All right then. Lead the way."

That smile made her heart miss a beat as they continued to walk along the sidewalk. Like she'd told him, she didn't live far and they arrived at her studio apartment in no time. "It's small," she said, opening the door. "But it's the right size for me."

She stepped aside and he entered. She immediately

thought her apartment might be just the right size for her, but with him inside it, it suddenly appeared small.

"Nice place," he said, glancing around.

Bristol was glad she was a neat freak. There was nothing out of place. "There's a bottle of wine over there if you want to pour us a glass," she said, removing her coat and hanging it in one of the closets.

"Okay," he said, removing his jacket. She took it and hung it in the closet, as well. She tried not to notice how perfect his abs were and what a broad chest he had. She also tried not to notice the sexual chemistry between them, which had increased now that they were alone and behind closed doors.

"Do you need to let your friends know where you are? Won't they be worried when you don't return to your hotel?" she asked him.

He shook his head as he grabbed the wine bottle and glasses off the rack. "No. They'll figure things out."

"Okay." She sat down at the table while he poured the wine into their glasses. And then he joined her there. "I know this isn't champagne but let's make a toast."

"To what?"

"To what I believe will be the best holiday I've ever had."

Deep down she believed it would be the best she ever had, too. Their glasses clinked and then they took a sip. She met his gaze over the rim and immediately, a deep sexual hunger flared to life in her midsection. From the hot, penetrating look in his eyes, the same hunger hit him, as well.

Bristol placed her glass down the same moment

he did. And then he stood and reached out to her. She went into his arms willingly and he lowered his head and captured her mouth in his. The moment she felt his lips on hers, a deep, drugging rush of desire filled her to the core.

He was using his tongue in the most provocative way, making shivers of need course through every part of her. She had never been kissed like this before and he was an expert.

He deepened the kiss and her mouth became locked to his. She couldn't hold back the moan that erupted from deep within her throat. Nor could she hold back the sensations overtaking her. She had been kissed before, but never like this. Never with this much possession, this much overwhelming power.

Moments later he ended the kiss and pulled back slightly to look down at her. A sexy smile touched the corners of his lips and the arms around her tightened, bringing her closer to him. "I wanted to kiss you from the moment I saw you. I had a deep yearning to know how you tasted."

Wow! She wasn't used to having such carnal conversations with a man. "Is that why you kissed me the way you did just now?"

"Partly."

"And the other reason?"

"I just wanted the feel of my tongue in your mouth."

And then as if he hadn't gotten enough of doing that the last time, he lowered his head and captured her mouth again. On a breathless moan she parted her lips, giving him the opening he needed. He slid his tongue inside, mating it with hers, over and over again.

When he finally released her mouth, she looked up

at him with glazed eyes. "What are you doing?" she asked, barely able to get the words out. Never had a kiss left her so off balance.

"Starting our celebration of the holidays."

She could feel blood rushing through her veins with his words. She hadn't expected this so soon. She figured they would share a drink today and then tomorrow he could come back for lunch. But it seemed he had other plans, plans she was giving in to. She couldn't help it. So many sexual sensations were taking over her mind and body just from his kiss. She knew there was no way she could stop from wanting him. He sealed her fate when he began kissing her again and she felt herself being lifted into his arms.

He was carrying her someplace and she knew where when he placed her on the bed. What happened next was amazing. In record time he had removed both of their clothes, as if needing to be skin to skin with her was paramount. As if needing to see her naked body was essential.

In a way she understood, since seeing him standing there without a stitch of clothing was doing something to her, as well. He represented such virility and masculinity, and coiling arousal was throbbing deep in her core. Never had she wanted to make love to someone so badly. Never had she felt this filled with need. And she could tell from his huge erection that he wanted her. His desire for her was obvious.

She watched as he put on a condom before heading back to the bed. She reached out and glided her hands up his tight, sculpted abdomen and chest, loving the feel of his skin. Heat curled inside her with the contact.

"You touch me and I will touch you," he warned,

grazing his jaw against her ear, while growling low in his throat. It amazed her that he would respond to her touch this way.

"I want you to touch me, Laramie."

She couldn't believe she'd said that. But there was something about Laramie Cooper that she didn't understand. Namely, how he could make her lose her common sense. How he could make her nerves dance and her brain race. How he had the ability to make her want to have things she'd done without in the past. And how he made her want him with a passion.

She needed to make him aware of something. Make him understand and she heard herself saying, "I've never brought a man here before."

She felt the intensity of his gaze all over her body.

"There's a first time for everything, don't you think?" he replied, slowly moving back toward the bed.

With each step he took, she felt her womb contract. He was staring at her with dark, penetrating eyes and her body heated under his intense regard. She'd never had a one-night stand in her life. Always thought she was above that. But at that moment the only thing she wanted was this man, who had the ability to mess with her mind and senses.

There was something else she needed to tell him and it was best if she did it now. "Laramie?"

"Yes?"

"I'm not on any type of birth control."

If she thought that revelation would stop him dead in his tracks, she'd been wrong. He kept moving toward her. "I have condoms. Plenty of them. Around a dozen or so. And if we need more we'll get them," he told her.

Get more? Did he honestly think they would use more than a dozen? Her heart began beating way too fast as she wondered just what kind of stamina he had. Would she be able to keep up?

She was about to find out.

He joined her on the bed and began kissing her again while touching her all over. Sexual excitement churned inside her, sending an intense throb through her veins. She slipped her arms around his muscled back, loving the manly feel of him.

"I'm dying to taste you," he whispered, just moments before shifting his body to place his head between her legs.

She gripped tight to his shoulders as she felt his hot tongue inside her, stroking and licking. He was unwavering in his determination to taste her like he wanted. Sensations she'd never experienced before rushed through her and instinctively, she made sinfully erotic movements with her hips against his mouth.

Over and over he laved her womanly core with greedy intent, making her whisper his name over and over. Suddenly, her body exploded like a volcano erupting and she surrendered to the pleasure he'd given her.

Before the last spasm left her body, he had shifted to position his body over hers, and then she felt him enter her, stretching her to accommodate his size. She inhaled the scent of him—the scent of them—and then used her tongue to lick his shoulder, needing to taste the texture of his skin.

He pushed his shaft as deep inside her as he could

go and then he locked their legs together. He began moving, thrusting back and forth, in and out. He established a rhythm that sent sexual undercurrents all through her body.

He looked down at her, held her gaze as he made love to her. She clung to him, holding tight to his shoulders as if they were a lifeline. His languid, deep, hard thrusts were driving her over the edge and making every nerve ending in her body zing brutally to life.

He threw his head back and growled her name as he continued to make love to her, indulging her with his words. Her skin sizzled where their bodies connected and the more he stroked inside her, the more her body awakened to the aching hunger he was feeding.

And then he called her name again. Together they were slammed with another orgasm. He gathered her in his arms, touched the side of her face with his fingers as they rode the tidal waves of ecstasy together.

The next morning it had felt odd waking up with a man in her bed. They had made love practically all evening, only to get up around eight and eat some of the soup she'd made the day before with French bread. Then they had gotten back in bed and made love all over again. All through the night.

No personal information was exchanged. None was needed. She knew the next three days would be considered one and done. Chances were, they would never see each other again. They were taking advantage of the now.

"You're awake?"

She glanced over at him and saw desire in the depths of his dark eyes. "Yes, I'm awake."

"Good."

He got out of bed to put on a condom then returned to her. "And what if I wanted breakfast first?" she asked, grinning.

He grinned back. "And do you want breakfast first?"

She shook her head. "No. I want you, Laramie."

And she did want him. She had to keep telling herself this was just sex and nothing more. When he left here the day after Christmas he wouldn't be coming back, nor would they stay in touch. The only thing she would have were her memories. Regardless, she could not and would not ever regret any time spent with him.

After making love that morning they dressed and went out to grab breakfast. He surprised her with his suggestion that they get a Christmas tree. That meant they had to purchase ornaments, as well. He refused to let her pay for anything. Like kids, they rushed back to the house and decorated the tree. Their tree.

Since most restaurants were closed for the holidays, she decided to prepare Christmas dinner for them. That meant grocery shopping, which she told him she wanted to do alone. She knew from their earlier shopping trip how he liked to spend money and she wanted Christmas dinner to be her treat.

When she returned to her apartment he was waiting for her. The minute she opened the door and glanced over at him, heated sexual attraction consumed them. She couldn't put her grocery bags down fast enough before he was ripping off her clothes, making love to her against the refrigerator.

He surprised her on Christmas Day with a gift, a beautiful scarf and a pair of earrings. The gift touched her deeply. He'd apparently gone shopping when she left to get groceries.

She surprised him with a gift, as well. A pair of gloves, since she'd noticed his were well-worn. He said he enjoyed Christmas dinner, but most of Christmas was spent in bed making love rather than eating.

The next morning, the day after Christmas, she awoke to find him dressed and ready to go. Ready to walk out of her life. She hadn't expected it to be so hard, but it was. She knew she had fallen in love with him. Not with the sex but with the man.

He kissed her deeply, wished her the best in her artistic dreams and thanked her for making this one of the best holidays for him, ever. And then he turned and walked out the door...without looking back.

She'd quickly gotten up and stood at the window to watch him leave. He'd called a cab and, as if he'd known she would be there at the window, before getting into the cab he looked over his shoulder, saw her, blew her a kiss and then waved goodbye.

She blew him a kiss and waved back. And as the cab drove away she knew at that moment that Laramie Cooper had taken a piece of her heart with him.

# Three

*New York, present day*

"I'm glad you guys are finding this entire thing amusing," Laramie said as he moved around the hotel room to dress. He had placed the mobile call on speaker while engaging in a five-way conversation with his teammates.

"Hey, Coop, we can't help but think it's pretty damn funny," Bane Westmoreland said. "I can just imagine the look on your face when you discovered what you were delivering to that member of the Security Council wasn't top secret documents like you thought, but her pet cockatiel."

Laramie couldn't help but smile as he slid on a T-shirt. "No, Bane, you can't imagine."

"Well, just think positive," David Holloway said. "You got a free trip to New York."

"Damn, Flipper, it's cold as the dickens here. I prefer California weather," Laramie said.

"Stop whining, Coop," Gavin Blake said, laughing.

"Kiss it, Viper."

And then he said, "Hey, Mac? You still with us? You're kind of quiet."

"I'm still here," Thurston McRoy said. "I'm trying to keep up with you guys and watch the game, too. In case none of you realized, it's Thursday night football."

That led to a conversation about their predictions for what team would make it to the Super Bowl. By the time Laramie had ended the call, he was completely dressed and ready to leave.

And go where? He figured that since he had a taste for a juicy hamburger, he would grab a meal at Xavier's. Flipper had recommended he dine there and said he wouldn't be disappointed.

A short while later, Laramie entered the restaurant and was shown to a table. It was busy and there had been a fifteen-minute wait but he didn't mind. This wasn't his first visit to Times Square, but he did note a lot of changes since he was here last.

"What would you like tonight?"

He glanced up at the waitress. No one could credit him with being slow and he immediately knew the double meaning behind her question. "A menu would be nice," he said, hoping that would defuse any ideas she had.

Maybe another time, but not tonight. He just wasn't feeling it. He chuckled and wondered if he was running a fever. There hadn't been too many times when he'd turned down sex. And there was no doubt in his mind the woman was offering.

"I'll make sure you get a menu...as well as anything else you might want," she said, smiling.

He smiled back. "Thanks. The menu will do for now and a beer."

She walked off and returned with the menu and his beer. "Thanks."

"You can thank me later." Then she sashayed off.

He wondered why he wasn't taking advantage of those curves and long gorgeous legs. His excuse had to be that this place sort of reminded him of that café in Paris. The one where Bristol worked.

Bristol.

He'd been thinking about her a lot lately. Maybe because it was around this time—during the holiday season three years ago when they'd met. Whatever the reason, Bristol Lockett was on his mind.

After his rescue from Syria, one of the first places he'd gone had been to Paris to see her, a woman he hadn't meant to ever see again. But something had compelled him to seek her out, only to be told by the manager of the apartment complex where she'd lived that she had returned to the United States a couple of years ago and had not left a forwarding address.

When he noticed the waitress looking over at him, he decided to place his order, eat and then leave. He wasn't up for any female company tonight and didn't want the woman to get any ideas.

An hour or so later, he left the restaurant a pretty satisfied man. The food had been delicious but he'd had a hard time deflating the waitress's flirtation. By the end of his meal, she'd all but placed her apartment key in his hand.

Instead of catching a cab back to his hotel room, he decided to walk off the hamburger and fries he'd eaten. Although he'd complained earlier about the cold weather, it really wasn't too bad. He'd endured worse. Like that time his team had that mission in the Artic.

He was about to cross the street when a sign ahead stopped him. It was an art gallery and the poster said:

## TONIGHT
## SPECIAL SHOWING OF ART BY BRISTOL

Bristol…

He shook his head. He was losing it. He hadn't thought Bristol was a common name. Was it?

What if it wasn't? Could it be his Bristol?

He dismissed the idea that Bristol was his. She was merely a woman he'd had a three-day fling with while relaxing in Paris before a mission.

Merely a woman he hadn't been able to forget in three years.

The name was unusual. He'd told her so when they'd met. He knew she was an artist. She'd shown him some of her art.

There was no way she could be here.

But then, why not? She was a New Yorker. He'd gathered that much from a conversation she'd had with Bane. Laramie hadn't asked her anything. His main focus had been sleeping with her.

What if the Bristol on the sign was the same Bristol from Paris?

His chest pounded at the possibility. He watched all

the well-dressed people getting out of their limos and private cars to enter the gallery. He glanced down at himself. Jeans, pullover shirt, leather jacket, Stetson and boots. Definitely not dressed to mingle with the likes of the high-class crowd entering the gallery. But at that moment, he didn't give a royal damn.

He had to find out if this Bristol was the same woman he hadn't been able to forget.

"Would you like some more wine, Bristol?"

Bristol glanced up at Steven Culpepper, forced a smile and said, "No, thanks. I'm fine."

He nodded. Looking over her shoulder, he said, "Excuse me for a minute. A few of my clients just arrived."

"Sure."

She let out a deep sigh when he walked off. Why was he hanging around as if they were together when they weren't?

She glanced around. There was a huge crowd and she appreciated that. A great number of her paintings had been sold already.

"I see Steven is quite taken with you tonight, Bristol."

She turned to Margie. "I wish he wouldn't be. He's barely left my side."

Margie lifted a brow. "And you see that as a bad thing?"

Bristol shrugged. "I just don't want him getting the wrong idea."

"Oh, I see,"

Bristol doubted it. Margie was determined to play matchmaker.

"A lot of the people here tonight are ones he invited. People with money. Need I say more?" Margie then walked off.

No, in all honesty, Margie didn't have to say anything. Steven had told her several times tonight just how many people were here because of him. It was as if he'd assumed Bristol would not have gotten anyone here on her own. Although he was probably right about that, he didn't have to remind her of it every chance he got.

"Hello, Bristol."

She turned to an older gentleman. His face seemed familiar and after a quick study of his features, she remembered him. "You're Colin Kusac, a close friend of my father's."

He smiled. "Yes, that's right. I haven't seen you since the funeral and the reading of the will."

That was true. Her father had named Colin as executor, and the scene hadn't been nice that day, especially when all her father had left her was revealed. Krista had accused Bristol of looking for her father only to get his money. Her stepmother had been wrong about that.

Her father had told her that he and Colin had attended high school together and over the years had remained the best of friends. Before Randall died, he'd also told her to contact Mr. Kusac if she ever needed anything. Since there was nothing she'd needed, there had been no reason to call him.

"How have you been?" she asked him.

"Fine. And you? I understand you have a son."

She wondered how he'd known that. She lived a quiet life and it hadn't been highly publicized that she was Randall Lockett's daughter. Although, at her father's request, she had taken his last name. At sixteen it had taken a lot of getting used to, going from Bristol Washington to Bristol Lockett.

Although she'd taken her father's name, she'd never flaunted it to influence her own career. And in the art community her father had used the pseudonym Rand, so very few people had made the connection anyway. However, over the years, people had mentioned how much her paintings resembled those of the renowned artist Rand. Although Margie was aware of her father's identity, Bristol had sworn her manager to secrecy. Bristol wanted to make it on her own and not use her father as leverage.

And now she was Bristol Cooper…

"Yes, I have a beautiful two-year-old son. His first name is Laramie, after his father. His middle name is Randall, after my father. He has the names of two good men."

"Randall would have liked that. He would have been proud of his first grandchild." Colin didn't say anything for a minute and then added, "I miss my good friend. He was there for me more times than not. When I first saw your work, I was taken back by just how much you and he painted alike."

She smiled, thinking how wonderful it was that on this very important night, although her father wasn't here, a man she knew to be his closest friend was. "Yes, we discovered that before he died."

"Randall was a gifted artist and so are you."

"Thank you."

"There's a beautiful landscape over there that I'm

thinking about buying. I wonder if you can tell me what inspired you."

She knew exactly which one he was talking about. It was the first painting she'd done after her father died and a lot of her pent-up emotions had been poured into it. "Certainly."

And then she and Colin moved toward the huge painting on the wall.


"May I help you, sir?"

Laramie wasn't surprised someone had approached him the minute he walked into the gallery. All he had to do was look around the room to see he seemed obviously out of place. He really wouldn't have to stay a minute longer if the man could answer one question. "The artist on the sign. Bristol. What's her last name?"

When the older man, who he suspected to be someone in charge, gave him a strange look, Laramie added, "I once knew someone by that name."

The man nodded his understanding. "Oh, I see. Her last name is—"

"I will handle this gentleman, Jazlyn," an authoritative voice said behind him.

Laramie didn't turn around. He figured whoever had spoken would make himself known soon enough. Besides, he hadn't liked the emphasis the man had placed on the word *gentleman*. As if he thought Laramie was anything but a gentleman. And what had he meant by "handle him"?

Laramie inwardly smiled. He would like to see that happen.

"Yes, of course, Mr. Culpepper." And then the older man walked off.

The guy who'd spoken came around to stand in front of Laramie and quickly sized him up. Laramie didn't have a problem with that since he was sizing up the other man, as well. And Laramie didn't like the arrogant glint in the man's eyes, like he assumed he was better than Laramie just because he was dressed in a designer suit.

A quick assessment told Laramie what he needed to know. The man was in his upper thirties, probably a Harvard or Yale graduate, a Wall Street type, most likely CEO of his own corporation.

"May I help you, Mr...?"

Evidently no one had explained to this man the proper way to introduce oneself. It wasn't by asking a question. Therefore, Laramie didn't intend to give his name unless this ass gave his. Besides, his name was irrelevant to what he wanted to know. "Like I was saying to the older man a moment ago, before we were interrupted—I once knew a woman name Bristol and was wondering, what is the artist's last name?"

The man's smile didn't quite reach his eyes. Who was this man and what business was it of his that Laramie was inquiring about the artist?

"I'm sure it's not the same person."

How the hell would you know? he wanted to say. Instead he said, "Let me decide that."

He could tell his response hadn't gone over well. The man's eyes darkened in irritation. Evidently, he wasn't used to being put in his place. "I won't let you decide anything. In fact, I'm almost certain Bristol doesn't know you."

Laramie was beginning to read the signs. This man was territorial. Evidently, there was something going on between him and the artist. "You sound sure of that, Mr..."

The man smiled. "Culpepper. Steven Culpepper. And the reason I sound certain is because I know Bristol. We are well acquainted."

"Obviously. So what's her last name?" He tilted his Stetson back to stare down at the man, wondering why Steven was giving him a hard time.

"What's the name of the woman you're looking for? Just in case you haven't noticed, you're drawing attention."

And he was supposed to give a damn? Laramie drew in a deep breath, tired of playing this cat-and-mouse game. The man was probably right, it wasn't the same Bristol, but there was something about this man's attitude that rubbed Laramie the wrong way. "Lockett. Her name is Bristol Lockett."

The man smiled. "Lockett? Then I was right all along. Her last name isn't Lockett."

"So what is it?"

Evidently tired of this conversation as well, the man said, "It's Cooper. Bristol Cooper."

Laramie frowned. He and the woman had the same last name? What a coincidence. But then there were a lot of Coopers out there. "You're right. It's not the same woman. Sorry I took up so much of your time."

"No problem. Let me see you out."

"No need. I know my way." Laramie had made it to the door when he heard it. That laugh.

It was a distinctive sound that could only come from one woman. He turned and glanced around the room. He didn't see her. Had he only imagined hearing her laughter?

"Is anything wrong?"

That Culpepper guy was back. Laramie looked at him. "Not sure. However, I'd like to meet the artist, Bristol Cooper, after all."

"That's not possible."

Laramie was about to tell the man that with him anything was possible, when he heard the sound again. His gaze sharpened as he looked around the room. The sound had come from another part of the gallery. He was certain he hadn't imagined it twice.

He began moving toward the sound, not caring that people were staring at him.

"Wait a minute! You need to leave now."

When Laramie kept walking, he heard the Culpepper guy call out, "Mr. Jazlyn, I suggest you call for security."

They could call for security all they wanted. He wasn't leaving until he made sure…

He entered another area of the gallery and immediately felt it…that undisguised pang of longing and desire he hadn't felt in three years. He swallowed hard against the deep yearning in his throat as his gaze swept around the room.

And then he saw her.

Her back was to him. She stood beside an older gentleman as the two of them studied a landscape. Laramie knew without even seeing her face that the woman was his Bristol.

He'd only spent three days with her, but he knew that body, even if it was now draped in a beautiful gown. There were a few curves that hadn't been there before, but he was certain everything else belonged to Bristol Lockett, right, front and center. Especially that shapely backside.

He remembered the feel of his hand on that backside as well as the brush of his fingers along her inner thighs. He felt an immediate tightening in his gut at the memory.

Every muscle in his body tensed as he quickly moved in her direction. When he came within a few feet of her, he inhaled her scent. It was the one he remembered from Paris. Hurried footsteps were headed in his direction. Security was coming. Let them come. But not before he made his presence known.

"Bristol?"

She must have heard her name but she seemed almost afraid to face him. And when she slowly turned, she looked as if she was staring at the face of…a ghost?

She took a step forward. She whispered his name. And then she crumpled.

# Four

Laramie managed to grab her before she passed out on the floor, sweeping her into his arms. People were staring, some had begun moving in their direction, no doubt wondering what the hell was going on.

"Put her down!"

He recognized Culpepper's voice. Laramie turned to see Culpepper flanked by several security guards and the owner of the gallery. Then suddenly a woman pushed through the crowd. "What happened?"

Laramie thought it was obvious but answered anyway. "She fainted."

"Fainted? How? Why?" She then narrowed her gaze at him. "Who are you?"

"Laramie Cooper."

"Laramie Cooper?" The woman gasped.

He wondered why hearing his name had such an

effect on the woman. "Yes, Laramie Cooper. I need to take Bristol somewhere to lie down. And I need someone to get a wet cloth."

"Wait a damn minute," Culpepper was saying. "He has no right to be here. Who is he supposed to be?"

He heard the woman whisper something to the bastard that sounded like "He's her husband."

Laramie wondered why the woman would make such an outlandish claim. He wasn't anyone's husband. Then he recalled what Culpepper had told him earlier. Bristol's last name was Cooper. Now he was more confused than ever and confusion was something he didn't deal with very well.

Suddenly, the older gentleman Bristol had been talking to said, "Will someone do as this man asks and get a wet cloth? Jazlyn, where is your office?"

"Right this way, Mr. Kusac."

"Kusac?"

Laramie ignored the flutter of whispered voices repeating the man's name as if it meant something. Even the woman who was moving ahead of them stopped to look at the man in awe. Who was this guy Kusac? Was he a celebrity or something?

Laramie moved quickly toward the back of the gallery while carrying Bristol in his arms. He recalled the last time he'd carried her, from her kitchen to her bed.

Entering the gallery owner's office, Laramie laid Bristol on the sofa. The man who'd been identified as Kusac closed the office door, only admitting the three of them along with the woman. Laramie couldn't determine who she was studying more, him or Kusac. There was a knock on the door and Kusac opened it.

Wet cloths were handed to him and he passed them over to Laramie.

"Is she all right?" the woman asked nervously.

"Yes" was Laramie's response as he began wiping Bristol's face with a cloth.

"By the way, Mr. Kusac, I'm Margie Townsend, Bristol's manager. I appreciate you coming out tonight and giving your support. You and Bristol seem to know each other."

"We do. I was a close friend of her father's."

"Oh." And then out the corner of his eye, Laramie noted the woman moving closer to him. "And are you really Laramie Cooper?" she asked.

He didn't take his gaze off Bristol as he continued to wipe her face. She was even more beautiful than he'd remembered. Her chocolate brown skin was smooth and soft. He'd always liked the shape of her lips. They had the perfect bow. He recalled kissing them. How he'd licked them with his tongue.

Bristol was three years older now. Twenty-five. But you couldn't tell it by her features. It was as if she hadn't aged at all.

She still was the most beautiful woman he had yet to meet.

He switched his gaze to the woman who'd introduced herself as Bristol's manager and who'd asked him a strange question. "Yes, I'm Laramie Cooper."

"B-but you're supposed to be dead."

Laramie frowned. Bristol must have told her that. But then, how had Bristol known?

Deciding he would get all the answers he wanted from Bristol when she came to, he said, "Yes, I'd been captured, and they presumed I was dead."

"And you decided to show up after all this time?" the woman snapped. "Fine husband you are!"

Before he could ask her what in the hell was she talking about, Bristol made a sound. She whispered his name just moments before her eyes fluttered open.

And then she stared up at him. Tentatively, she reached up and touched his face, as if to make certain he was flesh and blood. Tears fell from her eyes when she whispered, "You're alive."

He nodded. "Yes, I'm alive."

"But they told me you were dead."

He nodded. "They thought so for a while, before I was rescued."

"Rescued?"

"Yes. Almost a year later."

From the look in her eyes, he saw something was bothering her. Maybe it was the fact that she was using his last name and claiming they were married.

"We need to talk privately, Laramie," she said, barely above a whisper.

She was right. They needed to talk. He nodded and then glanced at the other two people in the room. Before he could say anything, Kusac said, "We heard." He opened the door. When Margie Townsend hesitated, Kusac said, "They need time alone."

Margie nodded. "Yes, of course." She then said to Bristol, "If you need me I'll be right outside the door."

When the door closed behind them, Laramie helped Bristol sit up. She drew in a deep breath and stared at him. "I can't believe you are alive."

Laramie didn't say anything. He was trying to make sense of what he'd learned and was failing miserably. He needed answers to help him understand. "How did you know I was supposedly dead?" he asked, sitting beside her on the sofa.

She nervously licked her lips. "I tried to find you. I sent you a letter, through the navy, and it was returned. A friend of mine knew someone who worked in the State Department. They checked into it and that's what I was told."

"When was this?"

"A few months after I last saw you."

He nodded. "I was presumed dead, so the person was right. I was rescued just days before Christmas the following year."

"That was a long time."

"Yes, it was." Only his close friends knew about the nightmares he'd had for months following his rescue. Nightmares he still had at times. His enemies had tried to break him and he'd refused to be broken. But their attempts had become lasting scars.

"Why were you trying to reach me, Bristol?"

Bristol drew in a deep breath, not believing that Laramie was alive, not believing that he'd shown up here tonight. How had he known where she was? Had he been looking for her? If he had, that would make what she was about to tell him easier. But what if he hadn't been looking for her? What if he had forgotten all about her and moved on? For all she knew he could be married, although there was no ring on his finger.

She studied his features. He was even more handsome than she remembered. He looked slightly older and there was a hardness in the lines of his face that hadn't been there before. Instead of taking away from his striking features, the hardness defined them even more. And the look in his eyes reflected experiences she couldn't come close to imagining.

Even if those experiences had changed him, it didn't matter. He still had a right to know about her son. His son. Their son.

He could accept it or question whether Laramie was truly his, but he had a right to know. How he handled the news was up to him.

Drawing in another deep breath, she met his gaze and said, "The reason I tried reaching you was because I wanted to let you know I was pregnant."

# Five

Laramie froze. He stared at Bristol. He'd heard what she'd said but he needed to verify it. "You were pregnant?"

"Yes," she said in a soft voice. "And you're free to order a paternity test if you need to confirm that my son is yours."

He had a son?

It took less than a second to go from shock to disbelief. "How?"

She lifted a brow, indicating she'd found his question as stupid as he had, but she answered nonetheless. "Probably from making love almost nonstop for three solid days."

They had definitely done that. Although he'd used a condom each and every time, he knew there was always the possibility something could go wrong. "And, where is he?" he asked, still trying to wrap his mind around the fact that he had a son.

"At home."

Where the hell was that?

It bothered him how little he knew about the woman who'd given birth to his child. At least she'd tried contacting him to let him know. Some women wouldn't have.

If his child had been born nine months after their holiday fling, that meant he would have turned two in September. Laramie recalled that September. Although it had been hard keeping up with the days while being held hostage, somehow he'd managed, by counting each sunrise. He'd been lucky to be held in a cell with a tiny window.

He hadn't known that while being a pawn in his enemies' game of life and death that somewhere in the world Bristol was giving life.

To his child.

Emotions bombarded him with the impact of a Tomahawk missile. He'd been happy whenever Mac became a father again and had been overjoyed for Bane at the birth of his triplets. And now Laramie was a parent, which meant he had to think about someone other than himself. But then, wasn't he used to looking out for others as a member of his SEAL team?

"Have you gotten married, Laramie?"

He frowned at her question. Marriage was the very last thing on his mind. "No, I'm still single."

She nodded and then said, "I'm not asking you for anything, if that's what you're thinking. I just felt you had a right to know about the baby."

He stared at her while conflicting emotions warred

inside him. She wasn't asking him for anything? Did she not know that her bold declaration that he'd fathered her child demanded everything?

"I want to see him."

"And you will. I would never keep Laramie from you."

"You named him Laramie?" Even more emotions swamped him. Her son, their son, had his name?

She hesitated, as if she wasn't sure how he would like her response. "Yes. His first name is Laramie and his middle name is Randall, after my father. I thought you were dead and I wanted him to have your name. So I named him Laramie Randall Cooper."

He didn't say anything for a full minute. Then he asked, "So, what's your reason for giving yourself my name, as well?"

Oh, boy. Bristol wondered why so much was happening to her tonight of all nights. When she'd left home she'd hoped for a great night for the showing of her work at the gallery. She hadn't counted on a lover—specifically, her son's father—coming back from the dead.

And now he wanted answers.

Although she knew he deserved to have them, she wasn't ready to tell him any more than she had already. She just wanted to go home and hug her son. Tomorrow, she would tell her son that the father he thought had become an angel was now a mortal.

She was about to tell him she was tired of talking for now when there was a knock on the door. "I'll get that," he said, standing.

She still appreciated the way he walked. Spine ramrod straight, steps taken in perfect precision with the best-looking tush she'd seen on a man.

When Laramie opened the door he practically blocked the doorway, but she heard Margie's voice. "How is Bristol?"

"I'm fine, Margie," she said. Thankfully, Laramie shifted aside so Margie could see for herself.

"Do you need anything?"

"No, I'll be out in a minute."

"No rush. Most of the people have left anyway. But the good thing is that all your paintings were sold. Tonight was a huge success."

Was it? As far as her manager was concerned, it had been a successful night. But Bristol saw beyond the money her paintings had earned. She saw the man standing by the door. Her heart slammed against her ribs. Already she was wondering what changes were about to be made in her life.

"And Steven is worried about you."

Bristol saw Laramie's body stiffen at the mention of Steven's name and wondered why. She became even more curious when he said, "Tell Culpepper she's fine and is in good hands. Now if you will excuse us, Bristol and I need to finish talking." He then closed the door.

How had Laramie known Steven's last name? Had the two of them met? If so, when?

Laramie slowly turned away from the door to stare at her. It was a good thing she was sitting down because her knees began shaking. The intensity of his gaze sent sensuous chills through her body. How was that possible when she hadn't seen him in three years?

The sexual chemistry that had drawn them to each

other from the first was still there. She wanted to deny its existence, but she couldn't. She wanted to break eye contact with him and look away, but she couldn't do that, either. She sat there and endured the moment, hoping it would quickly pass. It didn't. It seemed to extend longer than necessary.

She decided to use it to her advantage; checking him out wasn't a hard thing to do. He wore a pair of jeans, a dark blue pullover shirt, a dark leather jacket, a Stetson and boots. He looked like a cowboy, ready to ride off into the sunset. He seemed to have gotten taller and his body appeared even more fit. Was he still a navy SEAL or had he given it up after that mission that had obviously gone all wrong?

Her gaze moved to his shoulders. She remembered them well. She could easily recall how she clutched tight to them when they made love. How she would cling to them while he thrust inside her. What she remembered the most was that Laramie Cooper was a very physical man, filled with an abundance of strength and virility.

She sighed as her gaze returned to his too-handsome face and stared into his eyes. And she saw it again, that hardness. Pain he refused to show. Ravaged secrets. A wounded heart. A damaged soul.

He probably didn't want her to see any of those things, but for a quick moment, she'd seen them anyway. She wondered what he'd endured during those months when everyone thought he was dead. Would he share the details of that time with her if she were to ask? Was it any of her business?

He didn't say anything as he continued to study her as intensely as she was studying him. What was he seeing? Besides a few extra pounds she hadn't shed after her pregnancy. Some men would think of them as curves. She thought of them as a nuisance that wouldn't go away no matter how much she exercised.

"Are you ready to answer my question?" he asked in a deep, husky voice that seemed to resonate inside her. "Because I have even more."

She'd been afraid of that. She also knew they couldn't stay holed up in Mr. Jazlyn's office forever. She understood she needed to fill Laramie in on so much that had happened but now was not a good time. "I suggest we meet tomorrow and—"

"No. I need to know tonight."

Tonight? "That's not possible," she said, glancing at her watch because she needed to stop looking into his eyes. His dark gaze wasn't just directed at her, it was assessing her in a way she knew too well. During those three days in Paris, she had been able to—most of the time—interpret what he was thinking from his eyes. Namely, she knew when he was ready to make love again by the desire she would see in them.

"Why tonight?" she asked.

"Why not tonight?" he countered.

Drawing in a deep breath, she said, "My neighbor, Ms. Charlotte, is keeping Laramie and I don't want to get home too late."

He nodded. "And where is home?"

"Brooklyn."

He nodded again as he continued to stare at her. She couldn't help wondering what he was thinking. She found out when he said, "I want to see my son tonight, Bristol."

Why did him saying her name, no matter the tone,

make an unexplainable warmth spread through her? "It's past his bedtime and he'll be asleep."

"Doesn't matter. I want to see him."

She eased up off the sofa. "Why?" she asked, not sure she was ready for him to come to her home, invade her space and meet Ms. Charlotte, who was the closest thing to a family she had now. "Don't you believe me?"

"Yes, I do. I just want to see him."

It was similar to her father's wish when she'd first made contact with him. She hadn't known what to expect when she'd first spoken with him. To break the ice, her aunt Dolly had spoken with him first. By the time Bristol had gotten on the phone, he had been eager to talk to her. Nervously, she'd blundered out the words, "I'm your daughter." And he'd said, "I believe you and I want to see you." He'd flown out that same day from Los Angeles and in less than eight hours was knocking on her aunt's door.

Bristol studied Laramie. Noticed his stiff posture. Was he expecting a fight? Hadn't she told him that she wanted him to know about their child? "Fine, you can see him tonight. A private car is taking me home."

She nervously nibbled her bottom lip. There was something she had to tell him before they left the office. It was the answer to the question he'd asked regarding her use of his name. "And to answer your question about me taking your name."

"Yes?"

"Before leaving Paris, I had already made up my mind to name my son after you, first name and last. But I didn't want people asking questions about why we had different last names. My friend Dionne came up with the idea. She had a friend who was an assistant to a judge in Paris who was willing to help with our plan. We did a fake marriage license where I listed you as my husband. It was then filed with the courts in Paris."

He didn't say anything for a minute before he asked, "Giving birth to a child without the benefit of a husband drove you to do that?"

She looked away for a second to figure out how to make him understand. "Yes. More so for Laramie than for me." She paused. "My mom was a single parent and I never knew my father. All my life the stigma of being born illegitimate bothered me because there were those who never let me forget. I got teased a lot about not having a father. I know having kids out of wedlock is more acceptable these days, but still, I didn't want to take a chance and put my child through that."

Although her mother had never said so, Bristol believed it bothered her mother as well, not only for her daughter but for herself. While growing up, there had been organizations Bristol's mother had tried to sign up for that had rejected their application because they hadn't met what was considered normal family dynamics. In other words, she didn't have a father and her mother didn't have a husband.

"I assume your manager believes we're married. She practically accused me of deserting you and my child."

Bristol rubbed her hands down her face, feeling bad about that. "I'm sorry. I'll tell her the truth."

"Don't bother doing that. At least I know why she's been acting like I'm scum. And I also now know why that Culpepper guy was acting like an ass when I asked about you."

"Steven?"

"Yes, I take it he's your boyfriend."

Where would he get an idea like that? "No, he's not my boyfriend. Steven and I have never even gone out on a date."

Laramie held her gaze, apparently finding it odd that the man would act so territorial under those circumstances. "But he has asked you out though, right?"

"Yes, but I've always declined. He's not my type." She checked her watch again and then looked up at him. "Are you going to deny you're my husband? People might question you about it."

"Don't worry. I won't give your secret away."

# Six

When they walked out of the office, the first person Laramie noticed was Steven Culpepper and how the man's eyes narrowed when they got closer. If the guy had gotten word that Bristol's supposedly dead husband wasn't dead after all, then what the hell was he still hanging around for?

Laramie detected Bristol's nervousness. Did she think he would rat her out, expose her for lying about their marriage when he'd told her he wouldn't? He slowed his pace and she slowed hers. He glanced down at her. "You okay?"

"Yes. I'm just surprised to see Steven still here."

That made two of them. "You want me to ask him to leave?"

"No. I guess he was concerned. I see Mr. Kusac is

still here, too. I can understand his concern since he was a good friend of my father's."

Laramie didn't say anything. He recalled how people had jumped into motion when the man named Kusac had barked out orders earlier. Even the owner of the gallery was quick to do the man's bidding.

Margie left the group to walk toward them, a smile on her lips. "Well, did the two of you get things straightened out?" she asked.

Laramie answered before Bristol did. "Yes, and we're leaving."

The woman lifted a brow. "Leaving? To go where?"

Laramie was tempted to tell the woman that he didn't think it was any of her business, but Bristol answered, "I'm going home, Margie. Is the car ready to take me there?"

"Yes."

"Good." She then turned to Laramie and said, "I need to say good-night to everyone."

"Okay, let's do that."

Her eyes widened, probably in surprise that he'd included himself in the goodbyes, but she didn't say anything as he walked with her over to the three men. "I would like you to meet Laramie Cooper."

Laramie was sure it didn't go unnoticed how Bristol had introduced him. She hadn't referred to him as her husband. He figured these people assumed he was her back-from-the-dead husband, but she wasn't allowing anyone to presume anything about the nature of their relationship.

She thanked the owner of the gallery for hosting the event and apologized for all the commotion she'd caused by fainting.

Maurice Jazlyn waved off her words and said, "I would have passed out, too, had I thought my husband was dead and then he suddenly appeared out of nowhere."

Laramie didn't speak. If they were waiting for him to explain his absence for the past three years, they could wait on.

Then Jazlyn's face broke into a smile. "But then, I certainly can't complain since every last one of your paintings sold and you being here brought Kusac out tonight. It's been years since I've seen him."

"And I was glad to see him, as well," Bristol said, smiling at the man. "Thanks for coming."

Colin Kusac smiled. "Your first art show in New York—I would not have missed it for the world."

Then Bristol's attention went to Steven Culpepper. Laramie didn't like the vibes he was picking up off the man. He hadn't liked them from the first. "Steven," he heard Bristol say. "Thanks for inviting all those people here tonight. It was a nice turnout thanks to you."

"No need to thank me, but I'd like for us to meet sometime this week. Several of my clients here tonight were impressed with your work and want to see more. A few are willing to commission some of your future projects."

"That's wonderful! I'm sure we can arrange a meeting," Margie said excitedly behind them. "Just give me a call, Steven. I'll work out a date and time when Bristol is available."

A tight smile touched Culpepper's lips. "Yes, of course, Margie." Laramie had a feeling Culpepper had wanted a private meeting with Bristol and her manager had ruined those plans.

"I'll call you tomorrow to discuss your availability, Bristol," Margie said.

"That's fine," Bristol said, smiling. She then turned to him. "I'm ready to go, Laramie."

He nodded and took her hand, leading her toward the door.

"I don't bite, you know."

Bristol glanced across the back seat at Laramie and had to admit there was a lot of space between them. He might not bite but she could vividly recall a lot of other naughty things he could do with his mouth.

Jeez. Why was she remembering that now?

"I know you don't bite, but I figured you would want your space."

She thought the chuckle that ensued from his throat sounded way too sexy for her ears. "Is that a way of letting me know you like yours?"

She shrugged. "I guess I've gotten used to it." No need to tell him that she hadn't had another man in her life since him, serious or otherwise. After her son was born, he had become her whole world and there hadn't been room for anyone else. Some women needed a man to feel like a female; she didn't.

He didn't say anything for a minute and that was fine with her as the private car carried them through the streets of Manhattan and toward the Brooklyn Bridge. When they'd left the gallery she'd noticed the temperature had dropped. Forecasters had predicted a heavy snowfall before Christmas and with this cold snap being less than two weeks before Christmas, she could see it happening.

"Tell me about him. My son."

Laramie's words intruded into her reverie and she glanced over at him. The bright lights from the tall buildings they passed illuminated his features and she could see why she'd been taken with him from the first. Any woman would have been.

In Paris, Laramie Cooper had been handsome and charismatic all rolled into one. He was still handsome, she would give him that, but he had yet to unleash any of the charm that had swept her off her feet and into the nearest bed. But then she figured when a man was told he was the father of a child he hadn't known he had, his secret son, shock might put a damper on the charm.

Bristol settled her body against the leather seat. Talking about her son was one of her favorite subjects. "He's perfect."

There was that sexy chuckle again from him. "Besides that. How about starting off telling me about your pregnancy. Was it a hard one?"

She could vividly recall all nine months of it. "Not after my sixth month. I was one of those unusual women who had morning sickness in the morning and at night. I could barely keep anything in my stomach, and the smell of some foods would send me rushing for the nearest bathroom."

"Sounds pretty bad."

"I thought so at the time. I had planned to leave Paris in my fifth month but my doctor restricted air travel until I was better. I'd lost a lot of weight. I wasn't eating much and what I was eating my baby was getting. That's why it doesn't surprise me now that Laramie is a big eater."

"When did you leave Paris?"

"In my sixth month. I wanted my baby to be born in the United States. Thank God for online shopping and for Ms. Charlotte, who lives next door to my aunt. The house was cleaned out and baby furniture delivered, which made things easy for me when I finally arrived back in New York. Once the morning sickness stopped and I could retain food, I blew up overnight but the weight gain was mostly all baby. Laramie was born weighing close to nine pounds."

"And during all that time you thought I was dead."

He'd said it not as a question but as a statement. "Yes. I had no reason not to believe what the State Department had reported. A part of me wished I'd known more about you so I could reach out to your parents. I recall you'd mentioned they were alive but you never gave me any personal information about yourself."

"And you never gave me any personal information about yourself, either," he said. "Though I do remember you telling Bane you were from New York."

No, they hadn't exchanged any of those details. She doubted if it would have mattered anyway. It was not like he'd intended to one day pick up where they'd left off. There was no doubt in her mind that after he'd been rescued he'd gotten on with his life and hadn't given her a second thought.

"How did you stumble across me tonight?" She was certain now that he hadn't been looking for her.

"I came to New York on military business. After dinner I was headed back to my hotel room when I saw the sign at the gallery with your name. I figured there couldn't be too many artists with that name."

"So you came into the gallery on a hunch?"

"Yes, although I knew from the way I was dressed

I would stand out like a sore thumb. And then I encountered your Steven Culpepper, who—"

"He's not my Steven."

"He tried to paint the picture that he was. Appeared pretty damn possessive, too. He'd convinced me you weren't the Bristol I was looking for, but then I heard your laugh."

"My laugh?"

"Yes. I was less than a foot from the door when I heard you laugh. Twice."

She nodded. "Colin Kusac was sharing something with me about how he and my father used to get in trouble in high school."

"Your laugh is what let me know you were the same Bristol. I remembered it."

Those three days they'd spent together had been memorable in so many ways. And it hadn't been all about the sex. They'd had fun sharing breakfast in bed, sharing jokes. They'd even watched movies together. She had enjoyed waking up in his arms and going to sleep the same way.

Those memories were what had held her sanity together while she carried his child and believed he'd been lost to her forever. Those memories were what she'd remembered when the labor pains had hit. She'd drawn comfort from them.

The car came to a stop and she glanced out the window. She was home. The place she'd escaped to when she needed to heal from the grief she'd endured when she thought Laramie had died. It was the place where, months later, she had brought her son. Because her baby had been so large, at the last minute she'd had to deliver by C-section. Luckily, Dionne had made plans to be with Bristol as her delivery coach and ended up being a lot more. Her best friend was a godsend during the weeks following the delivery.

The first time Bristol had seen her son she'd been filled with so much love. She'd been given a special gift. She'd immediately noticed how much he looked like his father. It was uncanny. Her son's coloring, the shape of his eyes, the tilt of his mouth, had all come from the older Laramie. And the older her son got the more he looked like his father. Would Laramie notice? There was no way he couldn't.

"Are you okay, Bristol?"

She looked over at him. "Yes, I'm fine." A part of her wondered if that was true.

The driver came around and opened the door. Laramie slid out, and she couldn't help noticing how his masculine jeans-clad thighs slid with ease across the leather. Then he stood by the door and extended his hand out to her, to help her out.

The moment she placed her hand in his, she felt it. That spark, that tingling sensation she'd felt the first time they'd touched. She glanced up at him and met the darkness of his eyes and knew he'd felt it, too. Knew he was remembering.

Then she decided she wasn't fine after all.

# Seven

Laramie considered what had passed between him and Bristol a few moments ago. He was fully aware of the strong sexual chemistry that was still between them. Even when they weren't trying, they pushed each other's buttons. No surprise there. But what he found surprising was the intensity of what he'd felt from her touch.

Shoving his hands in his pockets, he turned to look at the line of brownstones, especially the one in front of them. The SEAL in him quickly surveyed his surroundings, took in every nook and cranny. It was a nice neighborhood of older well-kept homes on a tree-lined street with sufficient lighting. Even the sidewalks in front of the homes looked as if they'd been scrubbed clean. It was easy to see this was a block that took pride in their neighborhood.

He followed as Bristol walked ahead of him. Several live plants lined the steps to her front door. Had he told her how nice she looked tonight in that long, flowing black gown with a split on the side? The male in him couldn't help but appreciate how those curves filled out the gown. She was a beautiful woman and he could understand Culpepper's interest. What man wouldn't be interested?

She took the key out of her purse and looked at him. Had she sensed he'd been staring at her backside? "Nice neighborhood," he said, in case she had.

"Yes, it is." She paused. "I will have to tell Ms. Charlotte who you are, as well. She will be shocked."

He nodded. "She also assumes we're married?"

"Yes. The only person who knows the truth is my best friend in Paris. Dionne."

Laramie didn't say anything as she unlocked the door and opened it. Then she stepped aside. "No, after you," he told her. "I'm used to bringing up the rear."

She nodded and entered her home. He followed, closing the door behind him. Her place had a cozy air. It felt small and intimate compared to the monstrosity of a house his parents owned, where he'd grown up as a child.

He stood in a foyer with stairs on one side and a living room on the other. The lit fireplace reminded him of how cold it was outside. The heat in here felt good. She had decorated for the holidays. A Christmas tree sat in front of the windows and he couldn't help noticing that several of the ornaments were the ones he had bought for her in Paris. It made him feel good to know she had kept them.

"Nice place," he said, glancing over at Bristol as he removed his Stetson and placed it on a nearby hat rack.

"Thanks."

"I thought I heard voices. You're home."

An older woman came down the stairs and he figured her to be Ms. Charlotte. She smiled when she saw them. Then suddenly, the smile seemed to freeze on her face and she stopped walking to stare at him.

"Sorry I'm late, Ms. Charlotte. How was Laramie tonight?"

The older woman answered Bristol, without taking her eyes off him. "He was fine as usual."

It was then that Bristol said, "Ms. Charlotte, I'd like to introduce—"

"I know who he is," the older woman said, still staring at him.

The woman's words gave Laramie pause. "How can you know?" he asked, lifting a brow.

"Your son looks just like you."

His son looked like him? "Does he?" he heard himself asking.

"Yes, your spitting image," the older woman said.

"That's one of the first things I noticed after he was born," Bristol added.

The woman finally continued down the stairs. When she reached the bottom step, she said, "I know you're not a ghost, so I can only assume you weren't dead as Bristol thought."

Laramie stared into the older woman's eyes. He admired their sharpness. He had a feeling you couldn't hide much from those eyes. "No, I wasn't dead, although the government thought I was. I was missing in action for almost a year before being recused."

For some reason he felt he should provide her an explanation. She nodded and her lips creased into a smile. "I'm glad you came back alive. You're going to love that little boy up there. He's a sweetheart."

Bristol groaned. "You shouldn't say things that aren't true, Ms. Charlotte. You and I both know he's just gotten the hang of the terrible twos."

"Like I've always said, boys will be boys. I should know after raising four of my own." She then glanced at her watch. "Time for me to leave. I'm sure the two of you have a lot to talk about," she said, heading for the door.

She glanced back at them, specifically at Laramie, and said, "I'm glad you're here." The older woman then opened the door and closed it behind her.

Laramie saw Bristol was focused on the painting that hung over her fireplace. He'd seen it before. In Paris. In her bedroom. It had hung directly over her bed. She'd told him it was one she'd painted with someone. He'd been amazed how the beauty of the Point Arena Lighthouse had been captured so magnificently on canvas. The painting was so vivid it seemed that the waves from the Pacific were hitting the shoreline. He recalled visiting the actual lighthouse years ago with his parents.

"Bristol?"

She switched her gaze to him. "Yes?"

"Are you okay?"

She stood beside a lamp and the light illuminated her. He was thinking then what he'd thought when he'd first seen her. She was beautiful. In the bright light, he could study her. See more. Her dark hair was swept up and away from her face in a way that seemed to make her features even more striking. Especially with those earrings in her ears…

It was then that he remembered. He'd given her the earrings as a gift. It seemed the Christmas ornaments weren't the only thing she'd kept.

"You're ready to see him?"

"Yes."

She nodded. "He's asleep, so whatever you do, try not to wake him. Laramie can be a handful when awakened from his sleep. He doesn't like that very much."

"I won't wake him."

"Okay. Then follow me please."

She headed up the stairs and he followed, feeling his stomach knot with every step. This was crazy. He'd faced bitter enemies without flinching. Yet knowing that at the end of these steps was a child he'd helped to create had nervous tension flowing through him.

The moment they reached the landing she turned to him. "This way. His bedroom is next to mine so I can hear him at night."

He nodded, inhaling her scent. It was soft, subtle— jasmine. He recalled that was her favorite fragrance and for those three days they'd spent together it had become his.

He hung back when she opened the door and entered the bedroom. She turned on a small lamp. His gaze raked the room. It had bright yellow walls and a mural of zoo animals gathered around an image of someone reading a book.

Then there was the toy box in the corner. He smiled, remembering how he would pull all his toys out of the box at the beginning of the day as a boy, only to have to put them back at the end. His parents always had a full-time housekeeper and undoubtedly, she'd figured the more she taught him to do in his playroom, the less she would have to do.

He watched Bristol move toward the bed. From the doorway he could see the small sleeping form beneath the blanket. A mop of dark curly hair peeped out and he instantly recalled the pictures he'd seen of himself as a child with the same mass of curly hair. His parents hadn't given him his first haircut until he was about four.

When Bristol stopped by the bed, he moved to where she stood as blood pounded in his temples. He looked down and his heart stopped. Suddenly, he was bombarded with emotions he couldn't keep in check. He was looking down at his child. His son.

*His son.*

A son he and Bristol had made together during their three days of heated passion. Three days he hadn't been able to forget. Three days, the memory of which had helped him maintain his sanity when any normal person would have lost it.

He had expected to feel something. But not this. Not this overflowing of emotions filling him to capacity, taking hold of his mind and heart. He might not have been interested in fathering a child before, but the thought that he'd fathered this one had intense pride tightening his shoulders then spreading all the way down to his gut.

Since his child was lying on his stomach, he could only see one side of his face. That was enough. His mind rang out with the words… *He's mine. All mine*.

Um, not quite, he thought, glancing at the woman

by his side. His son was hers, too. That was a fact he couldn't forget.

She met his gaze. At that moment, something passed between them and this time it wasn't sexual in nature. It was an unspoken understanding that no matter what, this child—their child—would always come first. He understood and accepted the pledge.

"Does he sleep through the night?" he whispered. He had to say something. He wanted to know so much. He wanted to know everything.

A smile touched her lips. "If you're hoping he'd awake anytime soon, no such luck," she whispered back. "He usually fights sleep tooth and nail, but when he's out, he's out until the next day."

"May I come back tomorrow to see him? Spend time with him?"

She didn't answer. Why? All he needed was a yes or no, preferably yes. Instead, she whispered, "Let's go back downstairs and talk about it."

Talk about it? Did she think her answer would make him yell and risk waking up his son? What was there to talk about? This was his son. She'd said so. He'd believed her even without seeing all of him. Drawing in a deep breath, he hoped like hell there was not about to be any drama. The only true drama he enjoyed was of the SEALs kind.

He followed her out the door and back down the stairs. "Would you like a cup of coffee or a beer, Laramie?"

"A beer will be fine."

"I'll be right back."

In a way, he was glad she'd left him alone for a few moments to deal with all these emotions. Was she deliberately stalling? Would she try to deny him rights to his son? She'd said the reason she'd tried writing to him three years ago was because she'd wanted him to know`she was pregnant. He'd just seen his child. Now what? Did she expect him to walk away? Should he consider obtaining an attorney so he could know his rights as a father? All he knew was that his son had his name. Bristol even had his name, although they weren't legally married.

He rubbed a hand down his face. The hour was late. Was he overthinking things? If he was, it wouldn't be the first time. He was a suspicious bastard by nature. He rarely took anything at face value.

She returned with a beer for him and a cup of tea for herself. He remembered how she would drink a cup of tea every morning and every night before bedtime. He would get all turned on just watching how she sipped her tea.

"Let's sit in there," she said, indicating the living room. "Although I loved my studio apartment in Paris, it's nice to have more room here, especially with Laramie."

She sat down but he remained standing. Her calmness kicked up the uncertainty inside him even more. Was this when she would tell him he could have no part in his child's life or that he would only get whatever part she chose to give him?

He opened his beer and took a huge swig. The cool liquid felt refreshing going down his throat. He glanced over at her and saw she was looking at him. It was as if she wanted to say something but was too nervous to do so. In that case, he needed to just come out and squash whatever ideas were formulating in her head here and now.

"I asked you upstairs if I could come back tomorrow and you never gave me an answer. So I can only assume you have a problem with me doing so. In that case, I think you need to hear me out, Bristol."

He moved to stand a few feet from where she sat and met her gaze. "I want to see my son again. Every chance I get. I want to know him and I want him to know me. I want to be there for him. I want to be a part of his life. I'm not a man who will walk away from my child. I have rights as a father."

He paused before adding, "And just so you know, if you deny me those rights, I will fight you legally with every penny I have."

# Eight

Bristol knew she needed to do something before she began crying. Already it was taking everything within her to fight back the tears glistening in her eyes. She doubted Laramie knew just how much his words meant to her.

A part of her had known that she'd fallen in love with him during their holiday fling for a reason. Although she hadn't gotten to know him in the way she would have liked, in her heart she'd believed he was a man with character. A man of honor. A man who believed in doing the right thing.

When she discovered she was pregnant, letting him know had been automatic because of what her mother had done to her father. But Bristol hadn't known, until this very minute, how Laramie would feel about their son. Whether he would accept him or walk away. Even when he'd said he believed Laramie was his and had wanted to see him, there hadn't been any guarantees as to what his reaction would be. But she could not deny him the right to see his son and if he'd walked out the door after doing so, it would have been his loss. Not hers or her child's.

But from what he'd just said so passionately, he didn't plan to walk out the door. He wanted to be a part of his child's life…just like her father would have wanted to be a part of hers had he known about her sooner. Laramie Cooper was proving there were decent men out there. Just like her father.

Tears she couldn't contain any longer wet her cheeks. Why was she getting so emotional? Especially now? She blamed it on the fact that the man she'd fallen in love with three years ago, the man she'd thought was dead, was not only very much alive but was here, in her home, standing in front of her and accepting his child without any hesitation. Of course that didn't mean he wanted to renew a relationship with her or anything; she understood that. That was fine. The most important thing was that he wanted a relationship with his son.

"Hell, Bristol, you're crying over what I said? Just because I want to be a part of my child's life?" Laramie asked in an incredulous voice.

More tears she couldn't control flooded her eyes, and she saw both anger and confusion in his features. She wasn't handling this very well and now she had him thinking the complete opposite from what she was feeling.

"I need to get some tissue," she said, quickly getting up to go into her kitchen to grab a few. Moments later, when she returned, Laramie was standing in front of her Christmas tree with his back to her. His hands were shoved into the pockets of his jeans. She wondered if he'd noticed the ornaments. She doubted he would ever know how much she'd come to treasure them. How each time she looked at one she was reminded of Paris.

"Laramie?"

He turned around and met her gaze. She could tell from his stance and his brooding expression that he was still angry, even more so. She needed to explain and the only way she could do that was to tell him everything. "I think we need to sit down and talk."

The look in his dark, piercing eyes said that as far as he was concerned, there was nothing to talk about, but he nodded anyway. She took a seat on her sofa again, but he said, "I'd rather stand."

She wished he would sit down. Then she wouldn't have to stare up at him. Wouldn't have to notice just how well-built he still was. How sexy he looked in jeans and a leather jacket. And she wouldn't have to notice how his eyes were trained on her. But she said, "Okay, if you prefer standing."

The room was quiet but she was convinced she could hear the pounding of her heart. "I might have confused you about a few things, Laramie," she said. "I would like to explain and hope in the end you'll understand."

She paused before saying, "Growing up, I never knew my father. Other kids had daddies and I didn't understand why I didn't. It was just me and my mom. One day...I believe I was eight at the time...I asked her about it. I wanted to know where my daddy was. She got angry with me and said I didn't have a daddy, that I didn't need one and not to ever bring up the subject of a father again. Her words were final and I knew it."

Bristol picked up her teacup and took a sip although the tea had cooled. "It was only after my mother died when I was fifteen that I moved from Houston to—"

"You lived in Texas?"

"Yes. I was born in Houston and lived there until I was fifteen."

He nodded. "I'm a Texan, as well. I was born in Austin."

She nodded and then continued her story. "When Mom died, I moved here to New York to live with my aunt Dolly. She was my mother's only sibling."

Bristol took a breath and then continued, "It was only then that I got up enough courage to ask my aunt about my father. I knew nothing about him. I didn't even know his name. But Aunt Dolly did. However, my mother had sworn her to secrecy. According to my aunt, my father and mother dated while in high school in Dallas but he broke things off with my mom to pursue his dream of studying art in Paris. My aunt said he asked my mother to go with him, but she refused, saying she didn't want to live in another country."

"Your father was an artist, as well?" Laramie asked as he leaned against a bookcase.

"Yes." Now might have been a good time to tell him her father was the famous artist known as Rand, but she didn't. Her father's identity wasn't important to this story.

"Imagine how excited I was when I found that out. When I learned where my artistic abilities had come from. It also explained why my mother never wanted me to pursue my art. I guess me doing so reminded her of him. Once I found out who he was, I wanted to connect with the man I never knew. The man my mom had kept from me."

She took another sip of her tea. "According to my aunt, my mother never told my father she had gotten pregnant. He didn't know he had a daughter. The reason Mom kept it from him was because she resented him for choosing Paris over her."

She paused again before saying, "I convinced my aunt that I needed to see my father. To let him know I exist. She prepared me by saying that he might not want a child, that he might question if I was really his. Aunt Dolly didn't want me to get hurt. But I didn't care. I needed to meet him."

She recalled that time and how desperate she'd felt. "One of the men at my aunt's church was a detective with the NYPD. He tracked down my father and discovered he lived in Los Angeles. I made the call to my dad the morning of my sixteenth birthday. Aunt Dolly talked to him first, to break the ice and introduce me. Then she handed the phone to me."

"What did he say?"

No need to tell Laramie it had practically been the same thing he'd said when she'd told him about their child. "He said that he believed I was his and that he wanted to see me. To prove that point, he flew out immediately. In fact, he knocked on my aunt's door in less than eight hours." She smiled. "That was the best birthday present ever."

She fought back the tears that threatened to fill her eyes again as she said, "On that day, I began what was the happiest two years of my life. He told me that he wrote my mother but she refused to write him back. His letters were returned. She stopped all communication between them. When he returned to Dallas from Paris that first year for the holidays, he'd tried finding my mother but no one knew where she had moved to. Later on, he met someone else. He was still married to that woman when we met. They had two young sons. None of his sons were interested in art and he was glad that I was. We discovered we had quite a lot in common."

"Was he upset that your mom kept your existence from him?"

"Yes, very much so. He saw that as wasted years. Years when I could have been spending time with him. We tried to do everything we could together during those two years because that was all we had."

A bemused look appeared on Laramie's face. "Why was that?"

She swallowed, feeling the lump in her throat. "Because, although I didn't know it, my father was dying of cancer."

She drew in a deep breath as she held Laramie's gaze. "So as you can see, my actions regarding you and my son were based on my own experiences with my dad. That's why I wrote to you as soon as I found out I was pregnant. I didn't want to make the same mistake my mother made. You had a right to know about him, even if you rejected him. It would have been your decision. Your loss."

He didn't say anything for a minute. "I'm sorry about your father."

"Me, too. But we got to spend two years together. He made me feel so loved. So very special. He even asked me to change my last name to his, and I did. He also asked if I would come spend my last two years in high school with him in California. That meant leaving Aunt Dolly and I was torn about doing that, but she was fine with it and encouraged me to go. Although she never said, I think he confided in her and told her he didn't have long to live."

"And nobody told you?"

"No. Very few people knew about his condition. In his final days, I saw him getting weak and asked him about it, but he said he'd caught some kind of a virus. He only told me the truth during his last days. That's when he told me what was wrong and if I ever needed anything to contact Colin Kusac, his close and trusted friend." There was no need to tell him how much her father's wife had resented her presence and how mean she'd been at the reading of her father's will.

"So you ended up in Paris to study like he had?"

"Yes. He made that possible before he died. He wanted me to study at the same art academy." She had worked at that café in Paris not because she had to, but because she had wanted to. Her father had taken care of her tuition as well as provided her with a generous monthly allowance. Then there had been the proceeds from her mother's insurance policies. She had put all the money in a savings account. While growing up, her mother had taught her the importance of being independent and not wasteful.

"I had a wonderful father. I just wish I'd had more time with him."

Laramie didn't say anything for a moment, then he asked, "Do you resent your mother for standing in the way of that happening?"

She drew in a deep breath. "Not now, but for years I did. She wanted to hurt my father by keeping my existence a secret from him. She knew him and had known he would have wanted to become a part of my life, but she never gave him that opportunity. In the end, she not only hurt him but she hurt me, as well. I could never do that to my child. That's why I would never stand in the way of you developing a relationship with Laramie. I know the pain and heartbreak it could cause."

The only noise in the room was the sound of the logs crackling in the fireplace. "Thanks for sharing that with me, Bristol."

Telling him the story of her parents and her relationship with her father had drained her. Slowly standing to her feet, she said, "Now that we've gotten that cleared up, what time would you like to come meet Laramie tomorrow?"

An anxious smile touched Laramie's lips. "How soon can I come?"

She chuckled. "Laramie is an early riser so I'm usually up preparing breakfast around eight. You're welcome to join us if you like."

"I would love to."

She glanced at her watch. It was late. Almost midnight. "Do you want me to call you a cab?"

"No, I should be able to get one on the corner."

"Okay." She walked him to the door and watched as he put on his Stetson, while thinking how much more cowboy than SEAL he looked at that moment. "I'll see you in the morning then."

"Yes. In the morning. Oh, by the way, does Laramie have a favorite toy?"

She shook her head. "No. Like most kids his age he likes stuffed animals. He does have this thing for airplanes and he likes to color so he has a ton of coloring books. For his birthday one of Ms. Charlotte's sons, who also has a two-year-old, gave Laramie an electronic tablet. I'm trying to teach him how to play educational games on it."

He nodded. "What kind of tablet is it?"

Bristol told him the brand. Her heart missed several beats when Laramie stood in front of her, holding her gaze. As if to get her mind off what she was feeling, she thought of something. "It might get confusing with you and Laramie having the same first names. Can I start calling you Coop, or is that name restricted to just your team members?"

"No, it's not restricted so that's no problem."

"Good."

He shoved his hands into his pockets. "If there's a change of plans or if you need me for anything, you can contact me at the Marriott Hotel in Times Square. I'd like for you to have my personal number," he said, pulling out his cell phone. "What's yours so I can call you? That way you can have it."

She rattled off her phone number and when she heard her phone ringing in the purse she'd placed on the table earlier, she said, "I got it."

He nodded. "Now you have mine and I have yours."

She dismissed any significant meaning to that. He was merely providing her his number because of Laramie. "Good night, Laramie…Coop. I am so glad you are alive."

He smiled. "Me, too."

He stood there for a second, staring at her, before

saying, "Good night, Bristol. I'll see you in the morning."

He turned and quickly moved down the steps.

Laramie entered his hotel room, feeling a happiness he hadn't felt in a long time. In addition to that, a rush of adrenaline was pumping furiously through his veins. What were the chances of the one woman he thought he would never see again, the one woman he thought about often, the one woman who'd helped him retain his sanity while being held hostage, would be here? In New York? And that he would run into her?

Well, he hadn't exactly run into her, but the circumstances surrounding their chance encounter still seemed unreal. And not only had he found out he had a son tonight, but he'd seen him. What a feeling! It was exhilarating, and he couldn't wait to share it with the guys.

He glanced at his watch. It was late. Almost midnight. But he knew Bane, Viper, Mac and Flipper would be up. However, Bane had triplets and Mac had four kids Laramie didn't want to wake up. To be on the safe side, he would text the four to call him.

Laramie also knew he needed to contact his commanding officer to let him know he would be taking his military leave after all. He wondered what would have happened had he not been in New York tonight. No telling when his and Bristol's paths would have crossed, if ever. He'd already missed two years of his son's life and he didn't plan to miss any more.

At some point he also needed to call his parents to let them know they were grandparents. He wondered how they would feel about that. They'd never hinted one way or the other if they wanted grandchildren. They hadn't ever nagged him about settling down or marrying.

After sending the text off to the guys, he removed his jacket and hung it in the closet before the first call came in. He recognized the number as Bane's. "You okay, Coop?" Bane asked with deep concern in his voice.

"Yes, I'm fine. But I do have some news to share. Hold on, I hear another call coming in."

The others began calling and they connected to their conference number so they could all be on the phone at once. "Okay, Coop, what kind of news do you want to share with us?" Viper asked.

"Don't tell us the commander gave you another top secret job. Another cockatiel for you to deliver to some very important person?" Flipper teased.

"Maybe it will be a dog this time," Mac kidded. "Or maybe a pet monkey."

Laramie took their jokes in stride; nothing could put a damper on his mood. "I ran into Bristol Lockett here in New York."

"Bristol Lockett? That woman we couldn't tear you away from in Paris three years ago?" Viper asked.

"If I recall," Bane said, "you went missing for three days because you were with her."

"And we couldn't wipe that damn smile off your face for almost a month," Mac interjected.

"So how was the reunion?" Flipper asked. "She still look good?"

"Yes, she's the same woman, Viper. I didn't know you were missing me so much during those three days, Bane. I don't recall smiling for almost a month, Mac.

If I did, I had a good reason for it. And yes, Flipper, she still looks good and the reunion was great once she recovered from fainting."

"Why did she faint?" Bane asked.

Laramie settled down on the edge of the bed. "Bristol thought she was seeing a ghost. She'd assumed I was dead."

"Why would she assume that? Had she contacted your parents or something?" Viper asked.

"No. I never gave her any information about my family."

"Then why would she assume you were dead? No agency had the authority to release that information. Our mission in Syria was a top secret, highly classified covert operation," Mac said.

"Bristol tried writing to me and the letter was returned. She knew someone who had a friend at the State Department who told her I'd gotten killed in Syria."

"Someone breached classified information?" Flipper asked.

"The person who did it felt she needed to know. Like I said, she was trying to reach me."

"Why was she trying to reach you?" Viper asked.

Laramie paused before saying, "She wanted to let me know she'd gotten pregnant."

Everyone got quiet and Laramie knew why. They were trying to digest what he'd said. A smile touched his lips when he added, "Yes, what you're thinking is right. I have a child. A two-year-old son."

# Nine

"Hungry, Mommy."

Standing at the stove while preparing breakfast, Bristol couldn't help but smile. Each morning her son woke up in a good mood. Hungry, but good. It didn't matter that he usually had a bedtime snack. He evidently slept that off every night.

"Mommy is almost done, Laramie. Please color me a picture."

"Okay."

She'd discovered early that Laramie liked marking up things, preferably with his crayon. When her walls became a target, she'd purchased him a coloring book. Now it was the norm for him to color her a picture in the book while he waited for breakfast. And since he was home with her every day, she used any free time she had to teach him things. He already knew his primary colors, how to count to ten and since she knew fluent French, she made that his second language by identifying things in both English and French. So far he was mastering both.

She had just finished cooking the eggs when the doorbell rang. Laramie ceased his chatter long enough to say, "Door, Mommy."

Wiping her hands on a kitchen towel, she turned and said, "Yes, I heard it." And from the way her heart was pounding in her chest, she knew who it was. Laramie... Coop. "I'll be back in a minute, sweetie."

Refusing to acknowledge the fact that she'd taken extra care with her looks this morning, she headed for the door. Coop was here to see Laramie and not her.

Before opening the door, she looked through the peephole. There was no way on earth she could dismiss just how incredibly handsome her son's father was. With his striking masculine looks she found it hard to believe some woman hadn't snatched him up by now. He'd said he wasn't married, but he didn't say whether or not there was a special woman in his life. She tried to push the thought out of her mind; it wasn't any of her business.

Their only connection, the only reason he was standing on her doorstep a little after eight in the morning, was Laramie. And from the looks of it, he was bearing gifts. She had a feeling her son would be getting an early visit from Santa.

Inhaling deeply, she opened the door. "Good morning, Coop."

Bristol looked even more beautiful in the daylight. Today her dark brown hair was flowing down her shoulders. And although she wasn't wearing lipstick, she'd put something on her lips to make them shine. Another thing different from last night was her outfit. Today she was wearing a pair of jeans and a pullover sweater. Was it a coincidence or had she remembered him once telling her that red was his favorite color?

The color really didn't matter because the woman standing in the doorway was too stunningly beautiful for words. He drew in a deep breath and pulled in her scent. She was wearing the same perfume from three years ago, from last night. He tried to keep memories of their holiday fling at bay so he could focus on their son. But then how could he, when the result of that fling was why he was here?

He recalled Mac's lecture. Mac, being the oldest of the group and the one who'd been married the longest, had given him advice last night. If Laramie's only interest in Bristol was his son, then he needed to make that point clear up front. Mac had known a lot of men who hadn't. Because of that, the women in those relationships assumed romance and the baby were a package deal.

As he tried to regain control of his senses, it occurred to Coop that while he'd been checking Bristol out, she'd been doing the same with him. He cleared his throat. "Good morning, Bristol. I hope I'm not too early."

"No, your timing is fine," she said, stepping aside to let him in. "I just finished cooking breakfast. I hope you're hungry."

Boy, was he ever, and it had nothing to do with food. The moment she'd opened the door, he'd felt it. The sizzle of attraction had been bad enough outside, but now, within the cozy confines of her home, it was stronger than ever. Did she feel it, too?

"Yes, I'm hungry."

He couldn't recall ever being swept away by a woman except for once in his life. And she had been that woman.

"Good, because I've made plenty. Laramie is up and as usual for this time of morning, he's in a good mood."

"Is he ever in a bad mood?" he asked, placing the gift-wrapped packages on her sofa.

She smiled and he wished that smile didn't cause a stirring in his gut. "Yes, whenever he's sleepy and tries like the dickens to fight it. That's when he becomes cranky." She took in the numerous gifts he'd brought. "Looks like you went shopping."

He smiled. "I did. I was there when the gift shop at the hotel opened. I plan to do more shopping later today. It's hard to believe Christmas is in less than two weeks."

"Yes, it is."

They reached the kitchen and Coop stopped dead in his tracks. The little boy sitting at the table staring at him was a miniature of himself. The emotions he'd felt when he'd seen his son last night came back to hit him tenfold. Ms. Charlotte and Bristol were right. His son resembled him so much it was uncanny.

They shared the same skin tone, eye color and shape of nose, lips and ears. And then there was that mop of thick curly hair. Although Coop wore his hair cut low now due to military regulations, for years he'd worn it long, even during his teen years. His parents hadn't had a problem with it as long as he kept it looking neat. And he could tell, even though his son was sitting down, that he was taller than most two-year-olds. But then Cooper men were tall. He was six foot two and so was his father. His grandfathers on both sides had been six foot three.

"Who's that?" Laramie asked his mother loudly, pointing at Coop.

"It's not nice to point, Laramie." The little boy put his finger down but kept an I-am-sizing-you-up look on his little face.

"Laramie, this is your daddy. Can you say Daddy?"

"Daddy?" his son asked his mother, as if for clarification.

"Yes, Daddy."

The little boy nodded, looked back over at Coop and said, "Daddy."

Coop's heart missed a beat at hearing his son call him that for the first time. He watched as Laramie began waving his hand, and then said, "Hi, Daddy."

Coop waved back. "Hi, Laramie."

And then as if Coop was being dismissed, Laramie picked up a crayon and began coloring in the book in front of him.

"You can go ahead and sit down, Coop."

Laramie snatched his head back up and scrunched up his face and said, "He Daddy, Mommy. Not Coop."

Bristol smiled. "You, and only you, can call him Daddy. I can call him Coop. You call him Daddy. Understand?"

Laramie nodded his head up and down. "Yes, Mommy."

Then to explain further she said, "I can also call him Laramie."

Laramie's face scrunched up again. "But that's me."

"Yes, but his name is Laramie, too."

Laramie then looked at his daddy. "You got my name?" he asked.

Coop decided not to say it was the other way around. Instead he would let Bristol handle this since she seemed to know how much their son could understand. "Yes, I have your name."

"But Mommy calls him Coop so he'll know when I am talking to him and not to you. Okay?"

Laramie nodded. "Okay." He then went back to coloring in his book.

Coop moved to the table and sat down. That got his son's attention again. Laramie looked over at him and with a stern face asked, "Clean hands, Daddy?" And to show what he meant, he held his hands out in front of him. "My hands clean."

"Oh." Coop got the message and glanced over at Bristol. "Where can I wash my hands?"

He could tell she was fighting back a smile when she said, "There's a bathroom right off the living room."

He stood. "Thanks." He headed to the bathroom to wash his hands. He had a feeling his two-year old son planned to keep him on his toes.

"Be still my hormones," Bristol muttered under her breath as she watched Coop leave the kitchen and head for the bathroom. Today he was wearing a pair of khakis and a pullover brown sweater. She was convinced that no matter what he put on his body, he was the epitome of sexy. There wasn't a single thing about him that didn't start her heart fluttering and send her female senses into overdrive. Then there was that self-assured walk he'd mastered. The man was true masculinity on legs.

"Daddy gone?"

She glanced over at her son as she placed the plates on the table. Was that sadness she saw in his little eyes? Of course, she had to be imagining things since Laramie had just met Coop. He couldn't have gotten attached already. She'd known Laramie would like Coop since he liked everybody.

"No, Daddy went to wash his hands."

Laramie nodded and then said, "Good." He then added, "Me got clean hands, Mommy." And just like he'd done for Coop, as proof of how clean they were, he held them out and flipped them over a few times.

She smiled and said, "Yes, you have clean hands, Laramie."

At that moment Coop returned and sat back down at the table. "Daddy back," Laramie said, smiling.

Coop returned his son's smile. "Yes, Daddy's back."

"Daddy, want to play some more?"

Coop, who was stretched on the floor, wondered how one little boy could have so much energy. He glanced at his watch. It was almost noon. Had he been here nearly four hours already? Breakfast had been delicious and he'd discovered just what a great cook Bristol was. When he'd complimented her she credited her aunt for making sure her culinary skills were up to par before she'd left New York to live in Paris.

After breakfast he helped Bristol tidy up the kitchen, although she'd said his help was unnecessary. But he'd wanted to help. Laramie had sat at the kitchen table, ignoring them while he colored.

Afterward they had gone to the living room. They'd placed most of the presents under the tree but there had been a few he'd let his son open now. Namely, more coloring books. To give him time alone with Laramie, Bristol had gone upstairs to her studio and closed the door. He felt good knowing she trusted him to take care of Laramie.

For a two-year old, his son was pretty darn smart. He spoke in understandable sentences and even knew how to speak French. During breakfast Bristol would lapse into French with Laramie. Coop appreciated that fact since he himself spoke several different languages, including French, and he enjoyed conversing with them in the language.

"Play games, Daddy."

Coop pulled himself up and looked at Laramie. He knew that his son didn't know the true meaning of the word *daddy*. To him it was just a name, but Coop hoped when Laramie got older it would come to mean a lot more. He wouldn't be around his son 24/7 because of the nature of his work as a SEAL. But he would be with him every chance he got.

That meant after every mission, he would head to New York. It no longer mattered that he liked California's weather better. His son was in New York and that's where he intended to be.

"He hasn't worn you out yet?"

He glanced up and saw a smiling Bristol standing in the entryway to her living room. He chuckled. "No, not yet."

"Well, you get a break since it's lunchtime."

As if Bristol had said a magic word, Laramie jumped up off the floor. "Lunch, Mommy?"

"Yes, Laramie. Lunch."

He was about to race for the kitchen when Coop stopped him and asked, "Clean hands?"

Laramie's small eyes widened. He then looked down at his hands. "No."

Coop nodded. "Come on, let's wash our hands."

Bristol watched them go, walking side by side. Father and son. It was a vision she'd thought she would never see, and seeing it now pulled at her heart. She recalled the telephone call she'd made to Dionne last night, to let her know Laramie was alive. It had taken her a full hour to tell her best friend everything, including how she'd fainted.

Then Dionne had asked her some tough questions. Namely, how she felt about Laramie and if she still loved him. Bristol had to explain that of course she still loved him but now her fears were greater than ever. She had taken news of his death hard and the grief had been so deep she'd sworn never to get that attached to another person again. It seemed all those she loved eventually died. Her mother. Her father. Her aunt Dolly. Was that why she was sometimes overprotective with her son? At least Margie thought that she was.

The work Coop did was dangerous. He risked his life constantly. Most of the time his whereabouts were unknown because the nature of his work was highly classified. There was no way she could make such a person a permanent part of her life. She couldn't imagine going through that sort of grief again. He'd beaten death once but the next time he might not be so lucky.

Dionne had asked Bristol the one question she

couldn't answer. How could a woman stop loving a man like Coop?

She had no idea but she was determined to find out. She and Coop hadn't had a chance to sit down and talk, other than the discussion they'd had last night. She had no idea how long he would be in New York or what his plans were while he was here. He had said he wanted to spend as much time with Laramie as he could, and she didn't have a problem with that. She wanted her son to get to know his father.

She needed to get to know him, too. There was a lot of personal information about Coop that she wasn't privy to. She'd just learned last night that he was born in Texas. He rarely spoke of his parents but she knew they were alive. At least they had been alive three years ago.

"Mommy, hands clean now."

Coop and Laramie had returned. Now he was sitting high on Coop's shoulders with a huge grin on his face. "Okay, then, let's head into the kitchen for lunch."

Coop put Laramie down and as soon as his little feet touched the floor he took off toward the kitchen. He paused at the kitchen door long enough to look over his shoulder to say, "Come on, Mommy. Come on, Daddy. Laramie is hungry."

Coop burst out laughing as he walked beside her. "Did I imagine it or did he eat a huge breakfast a few hours ago?"

She chuckled. "No, you didn't imagine it. You'll find out just how much food he consumes. You'll never guess how much I spend on groceries."

He stopped walking and touched her arm. She

couldn't contain the surge of sensations that settled in the middle of her stomach from his touch. "I will help you with that."

She shook her head. "Thanks, but I don't need your help. I told you last night that I don't want anything from you and I meant it." All she wanted was for him to have a relationship with his son.

"I don't agree with that."

She frowned, detecting his anger.

"We'll discuss this later, Coop. When Laramie takes his nap."

Coop nodded. "Okay. Do you need help with lunch? I can fix a mean peanut butter and jelly sandwich."

"No, thanks, I've got it covered. Today it's tuna sandwich and chips. He loves anything with seafood."

"So do I."

Bristol wondered if it would be the same way with Coop and Laramie as it was with her and her father. They had discovered so many similarities. She headed for the refrigerator, trying not to notice Coop's sexy walk as he moved to the table, where Laramie was already seated. She couldn't push to the back of her mind how he'd looked stretched out on her living room floor with Laramie. He had made himself at home and removed his sweater. No man had a right to such a sexy chest covered only by a T-shirt. She knew SEALs stayed fit, but he seemed to be working overtime doing so. And she tried not to think about how comfortable it felt having him here in her home with them. It was as if he belonged.

Air was nearly snatched from her lungs at the thought. How could she even think such a thing? There was no way Coop could be a permanent fixture in their lives. At least not hers. He was only here because of Laramie. Had there been more between them, he wouldn't have just stumbled across her the way he had. He would have looked for her after his rescue. But he hadn't. That reinforced her assumption that their holiday fling had been just that, a fling. Afterward he had moved on and not looked back. She knew she'd been out of sight and out of mind. He hadn't expected or probably hadn't wanted to ever see her again.

Like she told him, they would talk when she put Laramie to bed for his nap. There was a lot she and Coop needed to discuss. She had to reiterate that she wanted nothing from him. Hopefully, that would put him at ease that she wasn't going to hit him up for child support payments. However, she had a feeling he would want to pay them anyway, just because of the responsible person he was.

But she didn't intend to let him.

They also had to talk about her fake marriage to him. They needed to resolve that. Yes, she thought, as she began pulling the items out of the refrigerator for lunch. They definitely needed to talk.

# Ten

Coop would be the first to admit that he'd been somewhat nervous upon arriving this morning, not sure of how his son would react to him. So far things were going great and he knew he had Bristol to thank for that.

As he settled back on the sofa, he thought about what she'd told him about her childhood. Specifically, growing up without knowing her father. And then only getting to spend a couple of years with him before he'd died.

After hearing her story, he wasn't sure what was worse. Having parents who were bitter toward each other or having parents like his who were obsessively into each other. If he had to choose, it would be the parents who were obsessively into each other. As far as he was concerned, her mother's resentment, bitterness and anger had only hurt Bristol. It was sad how one person's decision could change the lives of so many. He was glad Bristol had learned from her mother's mistake.

He couldn't help but smile when he remembered lunch. Laramie had cleaned his plate in record time. More than once, Bristol had to tell him to slow down so his food could digest. Coop hadn't been sure if Laramie knew what that meant until the boy began taking smaller bites of his sandwich.

It was obvious Bristol and Laramie had a routine. He hadn't put up a fuss when she'd mentioned it was time for his nap. Instead, he'd waved goodbye to Coop. But not before he'd asked if Coop would be there when he woke up. Before Coop could answer, Bristol had told Laramie not to expect him to be there because he had things to do. Was that her way of letting Coop know he was wearing out his welcome?

Hell, he hoped not. He'd placed a call to his commanding officer letting him know that he would be taking his holiday leave and would remain in the New York area. Like he'd told Bristol last night... He planned to spend as much time with his son as he could.

"I think he was asleep before his head hit the pillow. What did you do to tire him out?" Bristol asked, grinning as she returned to the living room.

He looked at her and thought those jeans she wore definitely displayed all her curves. Not all women could wear jeans and exude that kind of effect on a man. The kind that could shoot his libido into overdrive. The kind that made him remember, whether he wanted to or not, how things had been between them in Paris. How easily they'd connected. How insatiable their hunger for each other had been.

With effort, he brought his mind back to the conversation. Coop smiled. "He wanted to play hide-and-seek."

"Oops. I should have warned you about that."

In a way, Coop wished she had. Then he would have given his son restrictions about not hiding in certain areas. Coop hadn't set any rules, and Laramie had found a good place to conceal himself in his mommy's bedroom. He hadn't felt comfortable going into Bristol's room but since she'd left the door open he had seen enough to know it was neat as a pin and decorated in colors of mauve and gray.

And he had seen her bed.

It was the same one she'd had in Paris. Seeing that bed had made him recall everything they'd done and how they'd done it. It also made him realize that his son was conceived in that bed. Or it could have been the time he'd taken her against the refrigerator.

"How many times did you find him?"

Bristol's question interrupted his reverie. "Every single time."

No need to tell her that he'd had to coax Laramie out of his hiding place in her bedroom so he wouldn't have to go in there looking for him. That hadn't been easy. A promise to take him to the park one day soon cinched it.

He watched Bristol sit down on the chair and somehow she did it in a way that was a turn-on. He inhaled deeply, remembering for the umpteenth time that Bristol was off-limits. His presence here had nothing to do with her but everything to do with their son. No matter how many good memories he had of them to-gether, no matter how hard he'd tried to find her in Paris, and no matter how attracted he was to her now, the bottom line was that Laramie was his focus.

A relationship with his son was the only thing that mattered. That meant he and Bristol needed to talk about a few subjects they'd skirted around.

Deciding not to beat around the bush, he said, "So let's talk, Bristol."

He could tell she was nervous. But whatever they discussed would be with the intent of putting their son's needs before their own. Unfortunately, Coop had plenty of needs.

He hadn't bedded a woman since his last assign-ment nearly eight months ago. No particular reason he hadn't done so other than the fact he'd been too busy trying to hire more men to help run the ranch in Lar-edo that he'd inherited from his grandparents.

Cooper's Bend was his favorite place in all the world and when he retired from being a SEAL, he planned to move there and make it his permanent home. He could retire after his twenty years with the military, which was what he planned to do. He had less than ten years left. Six more to be exact, since he'd entered the mili-tary at eighteen and could officially retire at thirty-eight. Then he would become the full-time rancher his grandfather had been. In the meantime, he had a good group of people running the place and went there from time to time to check on things.

It might be a good idea for him to consider mov-ing there now. That would eliminate his need to find housing in San Diego to accommodate him and Lara-mie. The ranch, which sat on over six-hundred acres, was plenty big. He would love for Laramie to visit him at the ranch that held so many wonderful childhood memories for him. Hell, when his son got older, he could have his own horse.

"Yes, I think we need to cover a few things and come to an agreement," Bristol said, interrupting his thoughts.

"Okay. What do you want to cover?" he asked her.

She paused and then said, "I meant what I said about not needing anything from you where Laramie is concerned."

Already Coop knew that wouldn't fly. "I can't agree to that because Laramie is my responsibility, too. A responsibility I take seriously."

She opened her mouth to argue the point and he held up his hand to stop her. "Not negotiable, Bristol. It doesn't matter if you're able to take care of him yourself. What sort of man would I be if I didn't contribute to the welfare of my child?"

She didn't say anything and broke eye contact with him to gaze down at the floor. He knew she was thinking, probably of a way to counter what he'd said. As far as he was concerned she could think all she wanted, he wouldn't change his mind. As the only grandchild, he had inherited trust funds from both sets of grandparents. Also, his parents had established an endowment for him that he'd been eligible for when he'd turned thirty. He was yet to touch any one of them. In addition to all that money and the ranch, he was heir to RCC Manufacturing, Inc., a corporation founded by his parents over thirty-five years ago upon their graduation from Harvard. Considering all of that, there was no way in hell he would not contribute to his son's upbringing. In fact, he'd already left a message with his attorney to contact him. He intended to list Laramie's name on all his legal documents as his heir.

"I think we should compromise," she finally said.

He lifted a brow. "Compromise how?"

"You can provide for his future, such as setting up a college fund. I'll take care of any expenses for his well-being now."

Coop shook his head. "No. I still won't agree to that. I want to provide for my child's present and his future."

A frown marred her features. "Why are you being difficult?"

He returned her frown. "Why are you? Most men who father a child and are separated from them are required to pay child support."

"But usually only until they are eighteen. All I'm doing is asking you to start the support at eighteen."

He had news for her. He intended to take care of his child for the rest of his life. The trust funds he planned to establish for Laramie would assure that. The age of eighteen had nothing to do with it. He couldn't believe he was even having this conversation with her. Most women would want his monetary offering. Was he missing something here? "Can I ask you something?"

She nodded slowly, almost reluctantly, before saying, "Yes."

"You said you only met your father at sixteen. I don't know anything about him, but did he wait until you were eighteen to begin providing for you?"

She stiffened. "He paid my entire tuition at the art school in Paris."

Cooper figured tuition at that school hadn't been

cheap. "That's all he did? He actually waited until you were eighteen before doing anything?"

"Of course not."

"Then why would you expect me to? Evidently being an artist has you rolling in dough since you feel you don't need my help. That might be all well and good for you, but not for me. For me it's the principle of the thing. It's about doing my share in providing for a child I helped to create. So please don't ask me to consider doing otherwise."

Bristol's gaze held Coop's and she could tell from the determined look in his eyes that he would not back down on this. She wasn't privy to his income as a SEAL but she was certain he could use his money for better things…

Like what?

She drew in a deep breath when she suddenly accepted something. It was apparent that as far as Coop was concerned, nothing was better than taking care of his son. For Coop, it wasn't about the money. It was about taking care of his own. She'd gotten the impression three years ago that he wasn't extremely close to his family. But what she'd failed to realize was that her son was now his family and he wanted to not only be there for him but also contribute toward his wellbeing. For Coop, the contribution was essential. She got that now.

He'd been saying it all along, so why hadn't she been listening? Probably because, like her mother, she was determined to be independent and not depend on anyone for anything. She didn't have a problem with Coop being a part of his son's life physically, but she was trying to stop him from being a part of Laramie's life financially. Most men would have jumped at the chance to get out of paying some form of child support. But Coop wasn't one of those men.

Neither was her father.

And Coop was right. Randall Lockett hadn't waited until her eighteenth birthday to be a father to her. He'd immediately stepped in and, like a whirlwind, he'd changed her last name to his, bestowing upon her all the rights of being his offspring. He had taken her under his roof, adding her to his household.

She had enjoyed living with him in Los Angeles, even if it had meant moving out west, attending another school and making new friends. To her it had been worth it just to spend time with her father. He'd made sure she hadn't gone without anything. But the most important thing was the time they'd spent together. Nothing else mattered. Not the closet filled with new clothes, the private school or the international vacations. Not even the new sports car he'd given her.

"Okay, Coop," she finally said.

"Okay, what?"

She released a deep sigh. "Okay, we will share in the cost of raising Laramie."

"You don't have to sound so overjoyed about it."

She narrowed her gaze at him before she saw his lips tilt into a smile. He'd been teasing. Releasing another sigh, she said, "I'm not trying to be difficult, Coop. But when I had Laramie I knew he would be my entire world and that I would be the one he would depend on for everything. I thought you were dead. For the past two years, I've made it work. There hasn't been a decision I made without considering him. Even when I decided to quit my position with that magazine publisher to become an artist full-time. I'm doing okay financially."

No need to tell him about the ridiculously high commissions she received every month from her father's art. "I was raised by a single mother who worked hard and made sure we didn't waste money on frivolous things. I knew the difference between getting the things I really needed and denying myself those things I wanted that weren't essential."

She didn't say anything for a brief moment then added, "The reason I suggested you handle Laramie's future is because I think that's what upset my father the most with my mother...besides her keeping my existence from him. Knowing she hadn't adequately prepared for my future. I had to explain to him that it hadn't been her fault since there was no extra money to set up a college savings account for me. Mom was a teacher, not a six-figure-salary engineer. She had student loans to pay back. But still, we lived in a nice house in a good neighborhood. I thought we lived pretty good."

She smiled. "Mom said we were a team and always would be one. I was happy. I was content. At the time. I really didn't think of life being any better. It was years later that I found out just how complicated life could be."

Coop nodded. "Our son's financial well-being is something you don't have to worry yourself with anymore because I'm here to help." He leaned forward and rested his arms on his thighs. "There is that other item we need to discuss before I leave today, Bristol."

She lifted a brow. "What other item?"

He held her gaze. "The issue of our fake marriage."

# Eleven

Coop could tell from the look in Bristol's eyes that she'd forgotten about that complication. That was unfortunate for her, since he clearly remembered. A woman claiming to be your wife was something that pretty much got stuck in your mind.

"I told you why I did it," she said in a defensive tone.

He leaned forward. "Yes, you did. But that doesn't mean we don't need to talk about it. Spinning that tale might have been okay when you assumed I was dead, but as you can see, Bristol, I'm very much alive."

When she didn't say anything, he asked, "What do you think we should do?"

She shrugged. "Why do we have to do anything? It's not as if anyone knows the truth but my best friend,

Dionne, and her husband, Mark, who was working for the judge at the time."

"It's a lie, Bristol. And one thing about a lie, it can come back to haunt you when you least expect it."

She stood and began pacing. He watched her, trying to keep his mind on the issue at hand, but found it difficult to do so. Especially when her body was in motion. He should be noticing the sound of the wooden floor creaking beneath her feet or the way her hair brushed against her shoulders as she moved. However, he wasn't attuned to either of those things. Instead his total concentration was on her body. A body he remembered so well.

Coop couldn't watch her move those jeans-clad thighs without recalling a time he'd been between them. Recollecting a time when he'd tasted her. Touched her all over. He was so damn aware of every damn inch of her.

She suddenly stopped pacing and looked over at him. Why? Had she detected him staring? Should he sit there and pretend he hadn't been? He doubted he could, even if he wanted to. That would be trying to do the impossible where she was concerned.

"What do you suggest?" she then asked him.

Right now he thought about suggesting they go upstairs to her bedroom and get it on. Rekindle those days in Paris, if for no other reason than to prove he hadn't imagined it, that it had been as good as he'd remembered.

"There are only two options, Bristol. Either we pretend to get a divorce to end the fake marriage or we make the marriage real."

She came and sat back down. "There's absolutely

no reason to make the marriage real, so getting a pretend divorce sounds good to me. All that involves is us saying we're getting a divorce. No paperwork needed." A huge smile touched her lips. "Great! That was an easy solution."

"Not quite."

She lifted a brow. "And why not?"

The muscles in his jaw tightened. "Because in the end you'll emerge smelling like a rose, but I'll be the scumbag. A man who deserted his wife and child for nearly two years, and then who turns around and divorces her."

His harsh description had her lifting a brow, which meant she knew he didn't appreciate the position she was placing him in. "But I told you why I did it," she said.

"And now you want to take the easy way out."

Coop wondered why he was taunting her, especially when he truly didn't give a royal damn what people thought. They didn't know him. No, it wasn't the people he was concerned about. It was his son. When Laramie grew into manhood, what story would he hear about and believe? No matter how much quality time Coop would spend with his son, he ran the risk of Laramie one day wondering why he hadn't been there for them when it mattered the most. Hadn't Bristol said she'd wondered about it when she didn't know the real deal with her own father?

And, if he was honest, there was another reason he was suddenly thinking this way. It was about those memories he just couldn't shake. It was his attraction to Bristol that had been there from the start. This deep sexual chemistry they'd given in to in Paris.

He'd always prided himself on being a person who exuded total control. His SEAL friends often referred to him as the quiet storm. There was a coolness about him. Always calm. Always composed. Levelheaded to a fault. And beneath all that equanimity, he was watching, waiting, always on the lookout for the unknown. Considering the possibilities while fighting off the restlessness. But when he was provoked, all bets were off and he would kick ass like the best of them. Even more so. When pushed into a corner, he came out fighting.

What if at some point down the road Bristol met someone and decided to marry? How would that impact his relationship with his son? Would he have to stand in line for his son's attention? His affection? Was there a way to assure that didn't happen? Was he being a selfish bastard for wanting to make sure it never did?

"Coop?"

He blinked. Had he been staring at her while all those crazy thoughts rushed through his brain? And were they crazy? His steady gaze held hers. No, they weren't crazy. Irrational, yes. Crazy, no. There was a difference.

When she said his name again he answered, "Yes?"

"Are you okay?"

Now, that was a good question. Was he? To her he said, "I just realized how little we know of each other. How very little information was exchanged between us in Paris."

"We didn't do much talking," she blurted out. From the look on her face he knew she hadn't meant to say that. It didn't matter since what she'd said was true. Her hormones and his testosterone had been working overtime and the only thing they'd wanted to do was assuage the desire flowing between them. He hadn't wanted to know anything about her and she hadn't wanted to know anything about him. For those three days, pleasure had been the name of the game and they'd played it well.

"No, we didn't," he said. "And now we have a son to show for it. I want to get to know you."

"Why?"

"Because you are the mother of my child and there is a lot I don't know."

She lifted a chin. "Don't sweat it. The only thing you truly need to know is that I love him, will always take care of him and put his interests first."

He wondered if that was really all he needed to know. Maybe. Then maybe not. It had been one thing to arrive in New York a few days ago without a care in the world. His only thought had been how soon he could return to California. Now things had changed. He had a son. A real flesh-and-blood son. He also had a fake wife, who was the one woman he desired most. He could admit that no other woman had ignited his passion as quickly and as easily as Bristol.

Thoughts of her had sustained him. He recalled every single time he had touched her. How he had touched her. He remembered tasting her and how she'd tasted. How it felt to experience heaven while inside her. Their bodies locked together and hurtling into one orgasm after another.

"I'm not sure that's the only thing I need to know, Bristol," he said, finally addressing her earlier statement. "I need to know you."

She frowned. "No, you don't."

"Yes, I do. And you need to know me. Laramie needs to know me. He has grandparents that he needs to get to know and vice versa."

"I have no problem with that."

No, she might not. But would everything be on her terms? What if that guy Culpepper decided to come back around sniffing behind her the minute Coop was gone? His mouth pressed into a hard line at the thought.

"Can I ask you something, Coop?"

He looked over at her. "Yes."

"How do you feel about having a son? One you didn't know you had?"

He thought about her question, wanting to answer as honestly as he could. "I always liked kids well enough, Bristol. I get along fine with Mac's four. They call me Unclc Coop and all. But to be quite honest with you, I never intended to have any of my own because marriage wasn't on my radar. And having one out of wedlock was something I never intended to do. But now he's here. I've seen him and knowing he's mine and that you and I made him is so overwhelming. It's caused emotions I didn't think were possible to feel. It's not just about me anymore. Now it's about my child and you."

He saw the frown that touched her lips. "You don't need to concern yourself with me, Coop."

Boy, was she wrong about that. As far as he was concerned, she and his son were a package deal. The kind Mac had warned him about. But them being a package deal was Coop's choice, since it obviously wasn't hers. Nevertheless, he knew better than to try to convince her just yet. They would finish their conversation regarding their fake marriage later.

"When can I come back?"

"You're always welcome here, Coop. You're Laramie's father and like I told you, I would never keep you from sharing a relationship with him."

However, if she were to marry one day, a future husband might. He'd heard stories from Flipper about how one of his brothers had to constantly take his ex-wife to court for visitation rights. Just because this guy she'd married hadn't felt comfortable with Flipper's brother coming around whenever he'd wanted to see his daughter.

Coop didn't want to deal with that kind of problem. "I'd like to take you and Laramie to dinner tonight," he said.

"Dinner?"

"Yes, dinner. Is that a problem?"

"No, but other than McDonald's, I've never taken Laramie out to eat."

He liked the idea that his son's first time going to a restaurant would be with him. "There's a first time for everything, don't you think?"

Bristol recalled another time he'd told her that. It had been in Paris after he'd stripped her naked and she'd told him that no other man had been in her apartment before.

"So will you and Laramie have dinner with me tonight?"

"Where?"

"You pick the place."

She drew in a deep breath. Maybe going out to dinner wouldn't be so bad. "Laramie loves spaghetti and there's an Italian restaurant not far from here."

"I happen to like spaghetti, too, so that will work for me, if it works for you," he said.

"It will work for me if it's early. I need to have Laramie back here with a bath and into his pajamas no later than eight."

He nodded. "Will reservations at five o'clock be okay?"

"Yes. That's the time he usually eats dinner anyway."

Bristol was wondering why on earth she was paying so much attention to Coop's mouth when they should be figuring out details regarding Laramie. Why was she paying so much attention to his captivating eyes? To his masculine body? She saw men all the time but had never focused on any of those things. Why him? She knew the answer. Mainly because she knew how that mouth felt connected to hers.

She knew how it felt to be held within the scope of those eyes while desire streamed through her. And she knew all about that masculine body. How it felt to be beneath it. To feel the weight of it on her. To feel him inside her. Her breathing became choppy and she forced her gaze away from him.

"Are you okay, Bristol?"

Was she? She wanted to think she was, but honestly she wasn't sure. He'd been the last man she had slept with and now all those hot, delicious and wanton thoughts were trying to take over her senses. They really hadn't finished figuring out how to end their fake marriage. For some reason, she found the discussion draining and really didn't want to go back to it right now. There was no doubt in her mind he would bring it back up again.

However, there was something that had been on her mind since last night that she did want to discuss. "I'm fine, Coop, but there is something I've been wondering about."

"What?"

"Your friends. Those four guys I met who were with you in Paris. Mac, Bane, Viper and Flipper. Are they okay?"

A smile touched his lips. "Yes, they're okay. I'm surprised you remembered them."

"They were nice and—" she said, chuckling "—unforgettable. I liked them. I often wondered if they had gotten captured with you and if they'd lost their lives."

"No, in fact they were part of the team that rescued me. If you recall, Mac was married when you met him. He and his wife are doing fine. Bane and his estranged wife renewed their vows and Viper is married now."

"He is?"

"Yes, and happily so. Reminds us of that every chance he gets. Flipper is still Flipper. Happy-go-lucky and cheerfully single. Bane and his wife had triplets this year, almost six months ago."

"Triplets?"

"Yes. Two boys and a girl. They want a huge family so I guess you can say they're off to a good start."

"I'm glad they're all okay. When I got word that you'd been killed, I wondered about them. I take it the five of you are still close friends."

"Yes, and we're closer than ever. Even while I was being held hostage a part of me believed they would find me and get me out. And they did. We stay in contact even when we're not on a mission. I talked to them just last night and told them I had seen you."

"You did?"

"Yes. They remembered you, as well. I also told them I had a son. They're happy for me."

"Even though fatherhood wasn't anything you asked for?"

"Doesn't matter. I used a condom. Close to a dozen if you recall. Evidently one was defective. I regret that." He paused and then said, "But under no circumstances do I regret Laramie."

She nodded. "Neither do I."

He inclined his head and looked at her. Under his close scrutiny she was tempted to cross her arms over her chest. She could feel her nipples hardening. "I keep thinking that things could have been different. You could have made another decision and not had him," he said.

She knew what he was hinting at. "Not having him wasn't an option for me. I admit becoming a mother was the last thing on my mind, but when I found out I was pregnant I knew I would keep my baby. When I mailed that letter to you, I had no idea how you would respond. It really didn't matter. I was doing what I thought was the right thing by letting you know. I was prepared to go solo regardless."

"And now you don't have to because I'm here."

For how long? she wondered. He was still a navy SEAL and could get called away on a mission at any time. A mission he might not return from. She'd already had to deal with news of him dying once; there was no way she could go through it again. That meant she had to fall out of love with him. But how could she do that?

He had made it pretty clear that he wanted to see Laramie as often as he could. So she'd be seeing him often, too. In that case, how could she begin the process of removing him from her heart? There had to be a way and she was determined to find it. She had lost her mother, her father and her aunt. The three most important people in her life were gone. Now she had Laramie. She lived for her son and that would be enough.

"I'll leave now so you can get some things done while Laramie is taking his nap. I'll be back around four-thirty."

"All right."

She moved to walk him to the door, but he just stood there. Staring at her. More specifically, his gaze was fixated on her mouth. She saw it. Felt it. Her lips suddenly felt warm. Sensitive.

She knew she should turn away so her mouth wouldn't be the object of his focus. But the truth was, she couldn't. His assessing gaze was getting to her, and she couldn't do a single thing about it.

Bristol knew what he planned the moment he took a step in her direction but she didn't back up. She couldn't. It was as if she was rooted in place. Then he was standing directly in front of her. His eyes penetrating hers. His features fierce.

"I thought about you a lot, Bristol. During those eleven months while being held hostage."

His words made her heart flip several times. He had thought about her? "You did?"

"Yes. Thinking of you kept me sane…especially

during those times I was being tortured," he told her quietly.

Oh, God! Tortured? There was an intense searing in the pit of her stomach. She couldn't imagine what he'd endured.

"I would close my eyes and remember each and every time I made love to you. Every single time I kissed you. We shared a lot of kisses over those three days."

Yes, they had. They'd shared a lot of things, including their bodies. He hadn't been the only one who'd remembered, although her situation hadn't been as difficult as his by any stretch of the imagination. Every time her child, their child, had kicked or moved within her womb, she would think of him. Mourn him. Grieve for him. She would also thank him for giving her his child.

"I need to kiss you," he said in a husky tone, reclaiming her attention. "I need to kiss you as much as I need to breathe."

And she needed to kiss him, as well. That was the shocking truth. No matter how independent she wanted to be, she needed to kiss him. Her eyes were focused on his lips with the same intensity that his had been on hers. She needed to feel the heat of her body against his.

She was succumbing to everything male that he represented.

"As you wish," Bristol whispered. She was the one who made the first move, standing on tiptoe, leaning in close and placing her mouth against his.

# Twelve

Coop wrapped his arms around her and took over the kiss. The moment their tongues touched, getting reacquainted in the most passionate way, liquid heat seemed to spread through, burning him from the inside out.

His body leaped to life. He was now a man very much aware and filled with a yearning so deep it ached. Yet at the same time the yearning calmed the beast within him. Made him accept that Bristol could affect him in ways no other woman could.

He hadn't counted on her kiss being as greedy as his, her need just as insurmountable. Their tongues were mating in ways that sent a crackle of energy escalating between them. From the very first, he'd known she was different. He just hadn't known what role she would eventually play in his life. He had no idea that one day she would become the mother of his child.

He had given more of himself to her than he had to any woman. Even now he felt a need for her in every cell, in every pore. How could she get under his skin this way? To the point where he confessed to thinking of her while being held captive. Remembering her while being in pain. He'd never shared that much about one of his missions with anyone. There had been no one to tell. His parents hadn't wanted to hear the gory details. And he hadn't been able to open up to the psychiatrist the military had ordered him to see. Only his SEAL teammates had known the hell he'd gone through. And now Bristol knew. Not everything but enough.

They needed to come up for air, so he slowly ended the kiss, pulling his mouth away on a guttural moan. Still needing a connection, he used the tip of his tongue to lick her lips from corner to corner, before grazing his jaw against her ear.

He dropped his hands and couldn't recall at what point his fingers had become buried in her hair. Now it looked unruly. Sexy as hell. The sight of her kiss-swollen lips made him even more aware of how much he wanted her. Desire pulsed through him and he felt hard as a rock.

He took a step back, because otherwise he would be tempted to sweep her off her feet and carry her upstairs to that bedroom he'd refused to enter earlier. "I'll be back to get you and Laramie around four thirty."

And then he headed for the door. He came close to making it out without looking back. But temptation was too much. Overpowering. He stopped and glanced over his shoulder. Bristol was standing there looking more beautiful than any woman he'd ever seen. There was heat in her eyes.

A hungry throb stirred inside him and he drew in a wobbly breath before forcing himself out the door and closing it behind him.

Bristol released a breath before burying her face in her hands. What on earth had she done? What on earth had she started? That kiss had made her come unglued. No, she'd lost her composure long before that kiss. The intensity of her sexual need had begun to affect her the moment Coop had walked into her house that morning.

She could no more deny the carnal attraction between them than she could refrain from breathing. And today, just a few moments ago in her living room, they'd both unleashed pent-up, held-back desires. Her body knew him, desired him, ached for him. Closing her eyes, she felt a surge of yearning trying to take over her senses again.

Opening her eyes, she refused to let it. At that moment she heard her cell phone ring and wondered who was calling. Coop had her number. Would he be calling her? There was no way he'd made it to the corner already. Maybe he'd decided dinner wasn't a good idea after all and was canceling. If that was true then she agreed with him. Sitting in a restaurant across from him might push temptation to a new level. She wasn't certain if their son would be enough of a buffer.

Pulling her phone out of the back pocket of her jeans, Bristol saw the caller wasn't Coop but Margie. She quickly clicked it on. "Yes, Margie?"

"You okay? You sound kind of breathless."

She swallowed. Did she? "I'm fine."

"I called to see how things turned out with your soon-to-be ex."

Bristol frowned, confused. "My soon-to-be ex?"

"Yes. You can divorce him on the grounds of desertion, you know. I can refer a good attorney you can use."

"Desertion?"

"Yes. At least that's what I call it. You thought he was dead. Granted I understand the military made a mistake, but if he had cared anything about you—even if he didn't know about your son—you were his wife. He should have moved heaven and earth to find you. Showing up now after all this time won't cut it."

Bristol didn't like what Margie was saying. But then her manager didn't know the whole story. "Laramie and I have things to work out."

"What's there to work out? I talked to Steven and he's concerned about a dead husband reappearing. But I explained things to calm him down. I told him it was all a mistake and you would send your ex packing in no time. I assured him that there was no way you would hook up with Laramie again."

Frissons of anger ignited in Bristol's spine. Margie was believing just what Coop said people would believe about him. And it was all her fault. Furthermore, who gave Margie the right to tell Steven anything?

"Look, Margie, I have to go." It was either end the call or end their relationship, Bristol was just that mad.

Her manager didn't say anything for a moment, then added, "You sound upset, Bristol, and I hope it's not with me but with him. I'm aware you loved your husband. And I can understand you having feelings for him now. But I hope you're not thinking about tossing aside a chance with Steven for a man who didn't come looking for you."

Bristol lost it. "I don't know how many times I have to tell you that I'm not interested in Steven. Now goodbye."

She then hung up the phone.


Coop released a deep sigh the moment his hotel room door closed behind him. What a day. It had started out with him enjoying breakfast with his son and then it had ended after lunch with him kissing Bristol like he couldn't get enough of tasting her mouth.

He licked his lips. He still hadn't.

He never knew a woman's taste could mess with your taste buds and block out your other senses. But he had found out today. He just didn't understand it. Once he'd returned to his team to hang out for New Year's, after spending those three days with her, he'd been fine. She hadn't totally consumed his mind.

But he had thought about her...

And he had thought about her even more while being held hostage, because when your thoughts were filled with orgasmic pleasure it could erase the pain. The more those bastards tried to break him, the more he'd thought about Bristol.

Was that why he was so consumed with her now? He had thought about her so much that the memories of the time they'd shared in Paris were now a part of him? He rubbed his hand down his face. Maybe he was thinking way too hard.

He was removing his jacket when his cell phone rang. He recognized the ring tone. It was Bane. He pulled his phone from his pocket, chuckled and said, "With triplets, don't you have more to do with your time these days?"

Bane laughed. "No. That's where the benefits of belonging to a large family kick in. Everyone wants to help out. There haven't been triplets in the family since Quade's babies and everyone's excited. I couldn't tell you the number of visitors we've had. And more of them are planning to visit for the holidays. I told the family about your son. They're ecstatic and want pictures, so I need you to text me a few. You know the routine so get with the program."

Yes, he knew the routine. He had pictures on his phone of Mac's four kids. His phone was also filled with pictures of Bane's triplets. In the beginning, it seemed like Bane would text him a new picture every other day. Now it had decreased to only one a week. "No problem. I'm taking them to dinner and will take a photo then."

"I take it things are going well. I assume you had that talk you said you were going to have with her."

"Yes, I had it. She wasn't keen on the idea of sharing support for our son. I had to explain that I don't operate that way. She didn't like it but she finally gave in."

"That's good. What did the two of you decide about the fake marriage?"

Coop rubbed the back of his neck when he remembered that particular conversation. "Bristol doesn't want to be married any more than I do. But we have Laramie to consider now. She suggested we just tell everyone we're getting a divorce. That will release her from the fake marriage. She sees that as the easiest and simplest way out."

"Is that what you want?"

Coop dropped down in the wingback chair. "No. But then marriage isn't what I want, either. At least it wasn't until I met my son. At first I convinced myself being a single dad wouldn't be a big deal since I'd be gone on missions most of the time anyway. But then I began thinking about those times I would be around. What if she began seeing someone who didn't want me to have access to my child the way I wanted?"

"You can work out visitation rights with an attorney, so there shouldn't be any problems with that. Why do I get the feeling there's more, Coop?"

Because there was more. It was at times like this that a part of him wished Bane didn't know him so well. He, Bane, Viper, Flipper and another friend by the name of Nick Stover had gone through the naval academy together. Mac had been a SEAL several years before any of them. For the longest time, Mac had come across like the big-brother SEAL looking out for them, like he figured they couldn't take care of themselves. Over time they'd learned how to look out for each other. A few years ago Nick had given up being a SEAL to take a job with Homeland Security after his wife had triplets.

He, Mac, Viper and Flipper had wondered if Bane would do the same thing because of his triplets. But Bane had assured them he wouldn't. Whereas Nick and his wife didn't have any family to help out, Bane had more family than the law allowed. Bane's triplets were the third set born in the Westmoreland family.

There were Westmorelands all over the place. In several states, including Alaska.

Coop was close to all his team members but he and Bane shared a special bond because they'd been roommates at the academy.

"Yes, there's more," he finally said. "It's Bristol."

"What about her?"

"I'm more attracted to her than ever, man. She's beautiful. She's also headstrong, independent and a wonderful mother to Laramie."

"Sounds like you're falling for her all over again."

Coop leaned back in the chair. "To be honest, I don't think I ever stopped falling. I told you how she was constantly on my mind while I was in Syria and how those memories of us together were how I held on to my sanity."

"Did you tell her that?"

"Yes."

"And did you tell her that the minute the hospital released you to travel that you headed to Paris, hoping to see her?"

"No, I didn't tell her that. Maybe one day I will."

"Women like to know they were thought of. Remember how I kept all those cards and letters over the years for Crystal. It meant a lot to her."

He and Bane talked a little while longer. When they ended their conversation, he glanced at his watch. He needed to make another call, namely to his parents. He also needed to follow up with his attorney. Afterward, he would go to the hotel's fitness center and work off that delicious breakfast and lunch Bristol had prepared.

He thought about their kiss again. What he'd told

Bane was the truth. He was attracted to her more so than ever. Visitation rights with his son weren't the only thing he was concerned with. Visitation rights with his son's mother were also on his mind. The thought of her marrying someone else bothered him.

*If it bothers you so much, then maybe you should marry her yourself.*

*What the hell!* Why did an idea like that pop into his head? Anyone who knew him would attest to the fact that he wasn't the marrying kind. He liked his freedom. He enjoyed not answering to anyone but himself. He…

Loved his son.

His lips firmed in a straight line. Yes, he loved his son, but what did that have to do with desiring Bristol? Suddenly, he knew the answer. His love for his son affected everything. Even his son's mother.

He groaned in frustration. He had suggested the option of making the marriage real. She had immediately rebuffed it. At the time, it hadn't bothered him one iota. That idea hadn't been at the top of his list anyway.

So why was he thinking about it now?

Once again the answer was the same. He loved his son. Unlike his parents, who believed their love for each other weighed more than the love for their child, he didn't hold such beliefs. Although he'd seen his child for the first time only last night, more love than he thought he could ever have for any other human being had seeped into his heart and it was going to stay there.

He loved his parents. He loved his SEAL teammates as brothers. But the love he had for his child was so amazing that more than once today he'd had to pause to make sure he hadn't dreamed the whole thing.

That little face looked so much like him it was uncanny. Maybe the next time they would have a girl and she would look more like Bristol. Coop went still.

How could he even think what he just had? A daughter? With Bristol as the mother? Jeez.

He stood and began pacing. He was really losing it to even think such a thing. He needed to stay focused. The only person he needed to be thinking about was his son. But how could he think of his son and not think of his son's mother? The woman who'd given birth to him? The woman who made sure he got all the things he needed? The woman who was already teaching him a second language?

Hadn't he decided earlier today that they came as a package deal? But that had only been regarding financial support and nothing more. Hadn't it? Then why was he thinking all crazy? Why was he thinking beyond the financial to something even more? To marriage?

*Because she's the woman you want.*

*Want and not love.*

He knew love had nothing to do with it. Whatever feelings he had for Bristol were purely physical. That kiss today proved it, as well as the sexual chemistry surrounding them whenever they were together. That conclusion about the nature of their relationship didn't bother him and he doubted it bothered her.

Coop stood and checked his watch. He needed to go to the fitness center to work off his sexual frustrations, and he had plenty. When he arrived at her house to take them to dinner, maybe he would have worked some sense back into his brain.

# Thirteen

"Daddy is back, Mommy?"

Bristol couldn't ignore the excitement in her son's voice. He had been disappointed when he woke up from his nap to find Coop gone. The light had come back into his little eyes only when she'd told him Coop would be back and would take them out to dinner to eat spaghetti.

Laramie had jumped with anticipation when he heard the sound of the doorbell. Now he was right at her heels as she moved toward the door. He was ready and she didn't want to admit it, but so was she. Her lips were still tingling from her and Coop's kiss earlier and she hadn't been able to paint for thinking of him.

And that wasn't good. She needed to get more than a grip. She needed to put things in perspective. When she did, that kiss would be placed on the back burner, where it belonged.

Looking through the peephole, she confirmed it was Coop. He looked handsome, just like the Texan he was proud to say he was. She opened the door and tilted her head to look up at him. Before she could say anything, Laramie, who'd managed to squeeze between her legs, said, "Daddy, you left me."

Her son's words had been spoken with such heartfelt pain that she understood why Coop reached down and pulled Laramie into his arms. She stepped back for him to enter. She was amazed at how quickly Laramie had taken to Coop. Maybe it was a male thing. Maybe he would get attached to any man. She wouldn't know because he rarely saw other men. Ms. Charlotte's sons came around every so often and Bristol hadn't dated since Laramie was born.

"I'll get his coat so we can go," she said, when Laramie sat down on the sofa.

"No rush," Coop said, glancing at her. "We have time."

She started to tell him that he couldn't get all emotional whenever Laramie flashed those sad brown eyes at him. Besides, due to the nature of Coop's job as a SEAL, there would be plenty of times when Laramie wouldn't see him. It was not like this would be Coop's address. He lived heaven knew where. But not here.

She crossed the room to the coatrack to get Laramie's jacket and heard what Coop was telling their son. He was being as honest as he could. "There will be days when Daddy will have to go away. Sometimes for a long time."

"How long?" Laramie asked his father. "This long?" Laramie then stretched his little arms out wide.

"Maybe even this long," Coop said, stretching out his own arms even wider.

"Oh." A disappointed pout curved Laramie's tiny lips.

Coop gathered his son close. "Just remember, I will always come back."

Bristol stopped. She had gone along with everything Coop had said until now. But considering the type of job he did, he couldn't promise that he would always come back. How dare he make such a promise to Laramie?

"Where you go, Daddy?"

"Far away. To keep you safe."

"Keep me safe?"

"Yes. Always."

Of course Laramie had more questions but Bristol had heard enough. She grabbed his coat off the coatrack, determined that she would have a talk with Coop when they returned from dinner, after she put Laramie to bed.

"Here's his coat," she said, returning to the living room to hand the coat to Coop.

There was no need for her to try and put on Laramie's coat since he was determined to stick to Coop like glue. The thought didn't bother her and she wasn't filled with even an ounce of jealousy. There was enough of Laramie to go around for the both of them. She thought it was sad her mother hadn't thought that way when it came to Bristol's father.

"Ready?"

She glanced over at Coop as she buttoned up her own coat. "Yes."

"I rented a car for us to use," Coop said, picking up Laramie.

"Just to go to the restaurant? We could have taken a cab."

"I plan to be in New York for a while and figured I would need one for you and Laramie."

She frowned. "Why would you need it for me and Laramie? If we need to go anywhere, we can take the subway like we always do."

"Not while I'm around," he said, heading for the door with Laramie.

Bristol didn't move for a moment, trying to push feelings of annoyance away. She was not used to depending on anyone except Ms. Charlotte. She should just accept what he'd offered as a kind and thoughtful gesture and let it go. Besides, her mother had always told her to pick her battles. What was foremost on her mind right now was the lie he'd told their son a few moments ago—that promise to always come back.

"Are you okay?" Coop asked Bristol, after she opened the front door. They were returning from dinner and he was carrying a sleeping Laramie in his arms.

"I'm fine. Why do you ask?"

"You were quiet at dinner."

She shrugged as she closed the door behind them. "I think Laramie did enough talking for the both of us."

Coop couldn't help but chuckle. That was true. His son had definitely been the life of the party. Their waitress had fallen in love with him and had been surprised at how well he conversed for his age. Laramie had eaten all of his spaghetti and clapped his hands afterward, saying how good it was.

Keeping his word to Bane about sending a picture, Coop had given their waitress his cell phone and asked her to take one of them. At first Bristol hadn't wanted to participate, saying it was about him and his son, and that his friends wouldn't want her included. He'd dismissed that assumption by reminding her how much they'd liked her when they'd met her in Paris.

The picture was perfect. They had looked like a family dining out together, enjoying their meal and each other's company. In addition to Bane, Coop had texted the photo to the others. Within minutes, his phone had blown up with their responses. They all thought Laramie was a mini-Coop just as he assumed they would. They also thought Bristol looked good. Really good. And texted him to tell her hello. They also said how good the three of them looked together. Funny, he'd thought the same thing.

He couldn't help but notice how little Bristol had said all evening. Was something bothering her? He knew she hadn't been keen on him renting a car just to have it available for her and Laramie, but surely she wasn't upset because of that.

"You want him upstairs, right?" he asked to make certain.

"Yes. I need to undress him for bed," she said, removing her coat. "It's past his bedtime. He lasted longer than I thought he would."

Carrying their son, he followed her up the stairs, trying not to notice the sway of her hips and the curve of her backside. But he did notice. He was a man after all, and didn't intend to feel guilty about checking her out.

He placed Laramie on the bed then watched while Bristol removed his clothes and put him in pajamas. Laramie opened his eyes once and gave his mother a droopy smile. "Love you, Mommy."

"Love you back, Laramie. See you in the morning." She leaned over and kissed him on the cheek. Then he drifted back to sleep.

Coop felt like an intruder to what was probably a usual bedtime exchange between mother and son. An exchange he was witnessing for the first time, one he felt no part of. He would have loved to dress his son for bed. But he hadn't been asked. Instead, he'd been delegated to the sidelines.

Bristol then glanced over at him and whispered, "We need to talk."

There was something in her tone. Whatever she wanted to talk about, he wasn't going to like it. "Okay."

She moved out of the room and he followed. In spite of his mixed emotions while watching Laramie's bedtime routine, Coop enjoyed walking behind Bristol. She helped keep his libido healthy. He thought now what he'd thought a number of times before. She looked good in jeans. He wondered if his son's birth was the reason behind all those curves that now looked even more delectable to him.

"Coffee or beer?"

Bristol's question thrown over her shoulder drew his attention. He had a feeling he would need something stronger than coffee. Probably even stronger than beer, so he would take the alcohol. "Beer."

She kept walking toward the kitchen while he remained in the living room. With her no longer in sight, he turned his attention to the Christmas tree. He might be wrong but it looked like she'd added more ornaments than were there yesterday. The tree looked all bright and festive, recalling to his mind how perfunctorily the tradition was observed in his own family. His parents, or rather the housekeeper, put up a tree every year. And it remained up until New Year's whether anyone was there to enjoy it or not.

He couldn't help but recall his telephone call to his parents earlier today, to let them know about Laramie. They were surprised he'd been so careless with protection and his father had strongly suggested Coop get a blood test before claiming anyone. His mother had stated that if Laramie was truly his, then they would give the little boy all the love they'd given to Coop. He'd had to chuckle at that.

When his mother asked what was funny, he'd respectfully said nothing. They just didn't get it, but at this point in his life, he didn't care. His parents weren't going to change and he was used to their behavior.

A part of him wondered if he would one day find his soul mate, like his father had. Coop knew well the story of how his parents had met in college and fallen in love, apparently at first sight. He often wondered if his parents had really planned for him, although they claimed they had. One thing was for certain, if Coop ever did meet his soul mate, he wouldn't get so wrapped up in her that he wouldn't love with equal intensity any child they'd made together.

He drew in a deep breath. Why was he thinking about soul mates? As far as he was concerned, one didn't exist for him. Laramie would most likely be his only child. He was satisfied with that.

"Here you are."

He turned and Bristol handed him his beer. It was cold, but what he felt was the warmth of her hand when they touched. She had a beer for herself, as well. This was the first time he'd seen her drink beer instead of tea.

"I didn't know you drank beer," he said, tempted to reach out and touch that lone dimple in one of her cheeks.

"There's a lot you don't know about me, Coop."

She had him there. "What do you want to talk about?" he asked.

She moved past him to sit down on the sofa and, as usual, he watched her movements. He wanted to go sit beside her, but knew he shouldn't. For two people who'd made a baby together, they were as far apart as ever. He felt it. She was upset about something and he couldn't wait to hear what it was. He moved to sit down in the chair across from her.

"I want to talk about what you told Laramie."

He lifted a brow. "And what did I tell Laramie?"

The lamp in the room cast a soft light on her features. She wore her hair up in a ponytail with little curls fanning her face. He remembered her wearing a similar style three years ago. He'd taken the band out of her hair so it could fan around her shoulders. His fingers itched to do the same thing now.

"That you would always come back to him."

"I will."

She frowned. "You don't know that."

Now he was the one who frowned. "Do you think

I'd deliberately stay away after seeing him? After getting to know him? You think I'd shuck my responsibilities? Even worse—that I could stop loving him and forget about him?"

"That's not what I'm insinuating, Coop. You're missing the point."

He leaned forward, needing to study her expression. To try deciphering what the hell she was talking about. "So what is the point? Why don't I know that I will always come back to him?"

"Because."

He lifted a brow. "Because what?"

He watched her bury her face in her hands and draw in a deep breath before looking back up at him. The anguish he saw in her gaze made his insides clench when she said, "Because you could die."

Coop didn't say anything. Flashes of a time when everyone thought he had died, when he'd lived each day extremely close to death, filtered through his mind. He pushed the memories back and concentrated on the real fear he saw in Bristol's eyes. That was what he would address. "Yes, I could die. But so could you."

He saw the shiver pass through her before she lifted her chin. "Don't even try to compare what I do with what you do. I paint. You and others like you carry the weight of the world and all of the country's problems on your shoulders. You constantly put your life in danger, Coop. Do you deny that?"

He shook his head. "No, I don't deny it. But whenever I leave for any mission, I have every intention of coming back. Would you have preferred me to tell my son I won't be coming back?"

"No, but I wish you wouldn't make promises you

might not be able to keep. If anything ever happens to you, I will be the one who has to explain what happened."

Why were they talking about him dying? Thanks to his son, he had every reason to live, not that he'd ever taken life lightly. But now he had someone in his life who made living doubly important. "I think you're going to the extreme with this, Bristol."

It was clear his words angered her. "You think I'm going to the extreme? You aren't the one who got word while four months pregnant that the father of her child was dead. Dead, Coop. I thought you'd died like all the others."

He frowned. "What others?"

"It doesn't matter. I prefer you don't make promises to Laramie you might not be able to keep."

He stood, feeling angry now, as well. "Then I suggest you do the same. Stop telling him at bedtime that you'll see him in the morning. Anything can happen to you overnight. You could even die in your sleep."

She narrowed her gaze at him. "Stop being ridiculous."

His jaw tightened. "Then I suggest you stop being ridiculous, too. There are no guarantees in life. People die every day. When your time comes, there's not a damn thing you can do about it."

She took a step forward. Got in his face. "I guess of all people you should know, since you had a chance to beat death."

Not good, he thought, meeting her eyes. He wished she didn't smell so good and he definitely preferred her not standing so close. As if it had a will of its own, his gaze moved from her face to her body. She was beautiful even when she was angry.

"And just what are you looking at?" she all but snapped.

Since she asked, he had no qualms in telling her. "You. Did I tell you how good you looked tonight?"

# Fourteen

Bristol suddenly realized she might have made a mistake by getting in Coop's space. How had they gone from discussing his death to how good he thought she looked?

She angrily crossed her arms over her chest and then wished she hadn't when his gaze shifted to her chest. As if on cue her nipples hardened right before his eyes. She drew in a deep breath and took a step back. "I think it's time for you to go."

"Is it?"

"Yes."

"I thought you wanted to talk," he said, reclaiming the distance she'd put between them.

"I think we've said enough for tonight."

"Do you? Have you ever noticed we never seem to resolve anything when we talk?"

"And whose fault is that?" she snapped.

"Both of ours." A smile touched the corners of his mouth. "I agree that we've said enough for tonight."

"Good."

"No, Bristol, this is good." And then before she realized what he was doing, he pulled her into his arms and lowered his mouth to hers.

Shivers of pleasure, the kind she only experienced with him, shot through every part of Bristol. Her eyelids fluttered shut, too overtaken by desire to remain open. When Coop slipped his tongue into her mouth, tasting of the peppermint candy he'd been sucking on earlier, she shuddered. More enjoyable shivers ran up her spine. Sensations consumed her. When his hands wrapped around her middle, she was pulled close to the fit of his hard, masculine body.

When she felt his engorged erection nestled in the juncture of her thighs, she couldn't help but moan. How could they have been talking about serious stuff one minute and kissing the next?

Heated pleasure nearly melted her where she stood. She should be fighting to hold on to her sanity, but she couldn't. Even thinking of it was almost impossible. His assault on her mouth was sensuous and unhurried. It was mind-blowing. It had awakened needs long ago forgotten. And when she thought she couldn't possibly handle anymore, he deepened the kiss and new sensations overtook her.

Suddenly he broke away and she moaned in protest. Looking into his eyes she saw a naked desire that nearly tripped her pulse. Thickened the blood rushing through her veins. The air shimmered around them with sexual undercurrents.

"I want you, Bristol."

His words, spoken in a deep voice, stroked over her skin like a warm caress. Her breathing became as rapid as her heartbeat. And she knew at that moment that kissing wasn't enough. Especially now that they'd been reminded of how it felt to become so enmeshed in each other. Sexual excitement curled her stomach at the memory. It wasn't about love…at least for him it wouldn't be. For him, it was physical desire driving what was happening between them.

She, on the contrary, was driven by deep, never-ending love.

Two different drives. One final destination.

No need to deny what she truly wanted. "I want you, too, Coop."

As soon as the words left her lips, she was swept off her feet into strong arms and carried up the stairs.

Coop practically took the stairs two at a time with Bristol in his arms. He'd been unable to endure her form of passion any longer. Desire was clawing at his insides, making his need for her palpable. His need to make love to her was a pulsing, throbbing necessity he couldn't fight.

Entering her room, he went straight to the bed and placed her on it. Then he stood back and began removing his clothes while watching her remove hers. She pulled the sweater over her head and tossed it aside. He inhaled a sharp breath when he saw her breasts encased in a sexy black lace bra. Breasts his tongue had known and wanted to know again.

She unhooked the front clasp of her bra and his erection throbbed harder when the twin globes were freed. He'd always liked her breasts—their shape, size and texture. Coop was convinced if given the chance, he could devour those nipples 24/7.

He stopped taking off his own clothes just to watch Bristol finish taking off hers. He was mesmerized, captivated, so damn fascinated. When she removed her jeans, leaving herself only in undies, his erection got harder. She was wearing black panties that matched the bra.

Three words immediately came to mind. Gorgeous. Hot. Awesome.

"Is there a problem, Coop?"

Her voice snapped him back. He swallowed when he shifted his gaze to her face. "No, there isn't a problem."

"I was just wondering."

He didn't want her to wonder about anything. Especially about him being anxious to make love to her. He was convinced that somehow during those three days they'd spent together in Paris, Bristol had gotten into his blood. That had to be the reason he hadn't been able to forget her. The reason why thinking of her had kept him sane. What other reason could there be?

He quickly removed the rest of his clothes and then pulled out a condom from his wallet. He sheathed himself, knowing she was watching. It wouldn't be the first time she'd seen him do this and he didn't intend for it to be the last.

Bristol frowned when he got closer to the bed. Her fingers touched the scars that hadn't been there the last time they'd made love. From the look on her face he figured she knew where they'd come from. And then she did something he hadn't expected. Something that touched him deeply.

She leaned close and showered kisses over the scars. It was as if she wanted to kiss away any pain they might have caused him. When her mouth came close to his erection, he pulled back. He didn't want a reason to take off his condom. That was probably how she'd gotten pregnant the last time.

"I want to be inside of you, Bristol. I need it," he whispered hoarsely, climbing on the bed to join her.

"And that's where I want you, Coop," she said, wrapping her arms around his neck. "Inside of me."

Maybe she shouldn't have said that, shouldn't have so openly admitted her desire. Maybe she should not have been so brutally honest. But what else could she say when the juncture of her thighs throbbed for him? When her nipples were hard? When her heart was beating fast? When every nerve in her body shrieked with excitement and anticipation? When the moment she'd kissed his scars it was as if they'd become hers?

There was still a lot they didn't agree on and they truly needed to be downstairs talking instead of in her bedroom doing this. But then, maybe this was needed before they could have any sensible discussions. It was hard to sit down and talk like adults when said adults wanted to tear each other's clothes off, roll on the floor in front of the fireplace and mate like rabbits.

There was nothing that could hold her back from this. From giving herself to him like she'd done three years ago. So much had happened since then, but she didn't want to remember any of it…except for the birth of her son. That would always be a spot of joy in her life. But right now, at this instant, she wanted to be transported back in time. She wanted to experience once again how it felt when their bodies joined. When he proved to her just how much vitality he had. How much stamina.

When he showed her just how much he desired her. She could never get enough of that. His open display of need made sexual excitement curl her stomach. She felt light-headed with the effect of his masculine power.

"I plan to take this slow, Bristol."

His words had a shock effect to her system. Slow? He had to be kidding. She was so enthusiastic she was convinced that slow would kill her.

He touched her, using his fingers to unhurriedly skim across her skin, right beneath her breasts. His fingertips elicited sensations that made parts of her tingle. Lighting her up like a flame he intended to let burn gradually before sensuously snuffing it out.

The intensity of his gaze took her breath. She wasn't sure what emotions she saw in his penetrating look—except for one. The sexual vibes between them. They were stronger than they'd been in Paris. That was hard to believe because what they'd shared in Paris had been mind-blowing at minimum.

While his fingers were intent on driving her insane with lust, he increased her pleasure by leaning over and whispering, "I need to taste you."

She knew what he meant. He'd already kissed her. She knew he was referring to tasting her in another way. A way she remembered so well. A way that made the throbbing between her legs intensify. The one thing she remembered about Coop was that he never did anything without telling her beforehand, to make sure she was comfortable with what he wanted to do. He was not a man who exploited a woman's weak moments. There hadn't been any surprises in what he did, only in the magnitude of the pleasure his actions delivered.

She nodded. He took the motion as consent. Before she could draw her next breath, he lowered his head to her chest and slid a nipple into his mouth.

She purred. Of course he would start here, knowing exactly what he was doing to her and how he was making her feel. He was well aware that he could push her into an orgasm just from his mouth devouring her breasts. He'd done it before and, from the feel of things, he intended to do it again.

Suddenly, he pulled his mouth away and looked up at her. "Did you breastfeed our son?"

His question took her by surprise. "Yes."

He smiled as if the thought pleased him. She didn't have the mind to ponder why when his mouth went back to her breasts. Then, as if with renewed energy, he began sucking hard. Her womb contracted with every draw of a nipple into his mouth and her purr got louder.

She needed to touch him. She slid her hands over his shoulders and down his arms before bringing them back to cup the side of his face. Tingling sensations built between her legs. She was certain she was about to be pushed over the edge when he pulled back, lifted his head and said, "Not yet. Remember what I told you. I intend to make this slow so you can remember me for a long time."

She felt his body shift lower. Then he was touching her stomach, caressing it with gentle strokes. His hands moved lower and his fingers stilled when they touched the thin line of a scar.

"Because Laramie weighed so much I had to have a C-section," she said, explaining the bikini cut that was barely visible. Of course someone as observant as him would detect it.

He didn't say anything, but she felt his mouth when his tongue traced a path over the scar. He was kissing her scar like she'd done for his.

The air surrounding them became even more charged. And she was suddenly filled with so many emotions she felt completely out of whack.

Then he lifted her legs to fall over his shoulders while her hips were elevated with his hands. He nudged her knees open and then as if it was the most natural thing to do, eased his face between her legs and slid his tongue inside.

He kissed her with an expertise she found utterly amazing. His tongue went deep. It was thorough. And it was excruciatingly slow. It was as if he had all the time in the world to drive her mad with desire. The more she moaned, the more he tortured her, delving deeper with powerful strokes.

Then she had to fight back a scream when her body exploded into a gigantic orgasm.

Shivers ran through Coop as the thighs encasing his face quivered. He knew what that meant but he refused to stop. In fact, he needed to keep going because her taste was more potent now. Her taste was what he'd remembered, what he'd longed for, yearned for. His shaft throbbed with an urgency he hadn't felt since the last time he'd been with her.

He felt her tremors subside but he refused to let up. Doubted he could even if he wanted to. The taste of her juices flooded him with even more desire. When her thighs began trembling again, he knew she was reaching climax again.

When he'd seen that scar he had been filled with such profound emotion. They both had scars to show from their time apart. Hers had been a celebration of life, his had been a prologue to a death that never happened.

Those days were over. He was free and back in the land of the living. Back in Bristol's bed. The same bed where memories had been made before. The same bed where his son was created. Same bed, same woman.

He couldn't get enough.

When the last of the spasms wore off, Bristol wondered how she'd had mulitple orgasms so close together. Had she been that needy? That greedy? That hard up for sex?

If she'd just wanted sex she would have dated Steven, or any of the other men who'd hit on her over the years. But none of them had enticed her to open herself up this way. To invite them to her bed. To tell them she wanted them inside her. Only with Coop could she behave so boldly. And she knew why.

She was still in love with him.

Coop smiled down at her as his body straddled hers. Surely he didn't think she had the energy for another round of anything. Especially intercourse of the

most intense kind. She was so tired she would probably fall asleep in the middle. But then she'd had two
orgasms in less than twenty minutes. She owed him
something and would fake it if she had to. He deserved
his pleasure, as well.

She'd only faked it for one guy, her first time in
high school. With Coop she'd never needed to fake a
thing. He'd kept her blood pumping. Kept the primal
attraction between them so real that she'd been ready
whenever he'd been ready. She'd even been tempted
to wake him up for more. But not this time. There was
no way her body could endure another orgasm tonight.
But for him, she would pretend.

"You're not about to go to sleep on me, are you?"
he asked her, staring down at her.

She looked into his eyes and her body warmed
under his intense regard. She lowered her gaze to his
lips. Lips that were wet with her juices. Why did that
cause a deep stirring in the pit of her stomach? Maybe
it was because she recalled how his tongue had lapped
her into consecutive orgasms.

"Ready to taste yourself?" he asked in a low whisper.

Blood rushed through her veins. He'd never asked
her anything like that before. Taste herself? She knew
how he would do it and imagining it aroused her
enough that a low moan escaped her lips.

"Is that a yes?"

A sensual force seemed to overtake her. Where was
his sexual aura coming from? Hadn't she thought of
faking it just a minute ago? Now he was arousing her
all over again with mere words. Laramie Cooper was
too compelling for his own good. Definitely too sexy.

She should have known she couldn't fake anything with him because he had the ability to turn her on, even when she thought such a thing wasn't possible.

"Yes," she said.

Then he lowered his mouth to hers. The moment their lips touched, every hormone in her body crackled. She knew it was more than their combined tastes driving her over the edge. It was the masterful way his tongue dominated her mouth.

Her nerves did a pirouette, her brain sprinted and her stomach flipped.

He ended the kiss and looked down at her in a way that made moisture gather between her thighs. "You're ready for me again, Bristol?"

Yes, she was ready, even when she'd thought earlier there was no way she could go another round. Not only could she go, she intended to participate to the fullest and there wouldn't be anything fake about it. "Yes, I'm ready."

Her legs opened automatically, as if her body needed what he was giving. It had been three years since she'd done this and the last time had been with him. She slipped her arms around his neck and felt the large length of his erection touching her feminine mound.

Then he eased inside, inch by inch. His fullness encompassed her as he went deeper, filling her to the hilt. Her body stretched to accommodate him.

"You okay?"

She looked up and met his gaze. "Yes, I'm okay."

And honestly, she was. It was like a homecoming. The man she'd thought lost to her forever, the man she'd believed would never make love to her again, was doing just that. It was more than she could have hoped for.

"Thank you for my son," he whispered hoarsely.

And then he began moving while still holding her gaze, as if daring her to look away. She stared into his eyes while his body thrust inside her with a rhythm that released a sensual throb of desire in her veins. The sinfully erotic movement of his hips drew everything out of her, while at the same time demanding that she take as much of him as she could. Each hard thrust made her moan.

He kept moving at an unhurried pace, as if he wanted her to feel every single stroke. And she did. They were a perfect fit. She felt intense pleasure all the way to her bones. The undercurrent flowing between them was explosive, hot with passion of the most mind-blowing kind.

Her body moved with his. Her inner muscles tightened around him. Together they were creating a sensual heat like she'd never felt before…not even the last time. She'd thought nothing could be more powerful than what they'd already shared. Bristol was proven wrong.

Then he increased his pace, refined his strokes and pumped into her with a vigor that made her entire body respond. She exploded the same time he did, and he covered her mouth to keep the scream from her lips.

They seemed to flow into each other. Her hips were connected to his. Their bodies were perfectly aligned as they experienced the throes of ecstasy together. When he finally released her mouth, she drew in a deep breath and clung to his shoulders. They rode the waves of pleasure together.

Moments later, he rolled off her and gathered her in his arms. His thumb stroked her cheeks. The last thing Bristol remembered before sleep overtook her was whispering his name.

# Fifteen

Coop wasn't sure what awakened him, but he jerked upright in bed and glanced around before remembering where he was. Bristol's bed. He drew in a deep breath and rubbed his hand down his face before looking at the clock. It was three in the morning. The spot beside him was empty. He'd been sleeping so soundly that he hadn't noticed when Bristol got out of bed.

Where was she? He lay back down thinking she was probably in the bathroom. A few minutes later, when she hadn't returned, he got up and checked. She wasn't there. Had she gone to see about Laramie? Coop pulled on his jeans and left the bedroom to go to his son's room. He found his son sleeping, but Bristol wasn't there, either.

He was about to head downstairs when he heard a noise coming from the attic. He knew from playing hide-and-seek with Laramie that she'd converted the attic into her studio and that was where she did most of her painting. Was she painting this time of morning?

Coop walked up the six steps and found the door open. And there she was, standing in front of an easel. Was she wearing anything under that artist's cape? It was short and hit her at midthigh, which gave him a good view of her legs. She had a nice pair and like him, she was in her bare feet. He watched the look of concentration on her face. Her full attention was on whatever she was painting. Considering what they'd done tonight she should be exhausted. Obviously, she had a lot of energy.

She hadn't noticed him and he decided not to disturb her. Coop took in the room. It was huge. There were several built-in cabinets for her supplies. There was also a love seat, as well as a sink and counter that he figured she used as a cleanup station. The room had only one small window and he figured she wanted the least distractions possible while painting.

Coop was about to leave when he noticed several framed photographs on the wall. One was a photo of her and an older man. They favored each other and he figured the man was her father. He studied the man's features and tried to recall why he seemed so familiar.

Coop leaned in the doorway and recalled bits and pieces of what she'd told him about her past. Their son's middle name had been her father's first name. When they'd first met, her last name had been Lockett. He also remembered the story she'd told him about the two years she and her father had spent together before he'd died.

"That's a picture of you and your father, isn't it?"

His words had her swinging around so fast she almost dropped her paint brush. She released a nervous breath. "Coop, you scared me."

"Sorry," he said, entering the room. "I woke up and found you gone and wondered where you'd taken off to." It hadn't been his intention to stay the night at her house, but after making love that first time, they'd slept and had awakened to make love once more. Then they'd fallen asleep again.

She smiled over at him. "I didn't want to wake you. In addition to painting during Laramie's nap time, I often paint late at night when he's asleep." She then broke eye contact and glanced at the framed photograph. "Yes, that's my father," she said proudly. He could hear the love in her voice.

"Randall Lockett was your father."

She snatched her gaze to him. "How do you know that?"

He could see the surprised look on her face. Was her father's identity supposed to be a secret or something? "I recognize him. I'm familiar with his work thanks to my parents, namely my mother. She owns several of his paintings."

"She does?"

"Yes."

He glanced at her easel and back at her before saying, "I even met him once when he came to Austin for an art show to benefit one of my mother's charities. I liked his work. I should have made the connection in Paris with your last name being Lockett and the two of you having similar styles. But it never crossed my mind." There was no need to tell her that the only thing that had been on his mind was getting her to the nearest bed.

"I can't believe you actually met my father."

He heard the excitement in her voice. "Yes, I was seventeen at the time and a senior in high school. It was the last event my mother sort of forced me to attend with her and my dad. In the end, I'm glad I went. He was a nice man. Very personable. Like I said, Mom has quite a few of your father's paintings and it was nice meeting the man who was getting so much of her money. I'm sure you know his work isn't cheap."

She chuckled. "Yes, I know."

"I remember that time well," he said. "I'd gotten word a few days before of my acceptance into the naval academy and was going away with my parents' blessing. I was relieved they hadn't placed any pressure on me to follow in their footsteps and take part in the family business."

"And what business is that?"

"RCC Manufacturing Company."

She lifted a brow. "RCC? I'm familiar with them. They're a huge operation based in Texas. I order a number of my art supplies through them."

He chuckled. "My parents would be happy to hear that."

"And you decided to become a SEAL instead of going into your family business?"

"Yes, that's right. I knew early on I wasn't cut out for the business-suit-and-tie crowd."

Coop glanced back over at the framed photograph and then back at her. "You seemed surprised that I knew Randall Lockett was your father, like it was supposed to be a secret or something. Was it?"

* * *

Bristol looked away from Coop to glance at the picture she'd taken with her father, one that she'd proudly hung on her wall. She wished Coop wouldn't stand there shirtless and in his bare feet. In jeans riding low on his hips and not quite zipped up all the way, with the snap undone. He looked way too sexy for her peace of mind.

She'd yet to answer Coop's question and she realized how little they knew about each other, even with all the intimacy they'd shared. She blamed it on the fact that whenever they were together they did little talking due to all the sexual chemistry surrounding them. Like now. She could feel it and she knew he did, as well.

She hadn't known so much need had been bottled up inside her. All it had taken was Coop unleashing it and she'd become a mad woman wanting to make up for lost time. Luckily for her, he'd been the same way. It was as if they hadn't been able to get enough of each other.

"It's not a secret per se. I just don't go around broadcasting it, so few people know. I don't want to use his name to build my own career as an artist, although I am proud to have been Randall Lockett's daughter."

"And I'm sure he was glad he was Bristol Lockett's father."

His words made her feel good. More than once, her father had told her how proud he was of her and all she'd accomplished. "Thank you for saying that."

"No need to thank me."

He moved around the room, looking at the easels showing various paintings she had done. She wasn't used to anyone invading her space, especially in here. For some reason his presence didn't bother her.

Another thing that didn't bother her, when maybe it should have, was how quickly they'd become intimate again. Had it been just the night before when he'd shown up at the gallery? She had wanted him immediately. Had needed him sexually. And he'd delivered, satisfying her.

It wasn't his fault that she had fallen in love with him years ago. Nor was it any of his concern that she was trying to fall out of love with him now. Sleeping with him hadn't confused the issue for her. She knew he didn't love her back.

She needed to get her mind off Coop, namely off his body, and transfer her thoughts to something else. She walked over to the coffeepot she kept in her studio and poured a cup. She then turned to him. "Would you like some?"

Her insides heated when his gaze roamed over her, making her realize just what she'd asked. She swallowed, thinking he'd had some already. A lot actually. But if he wanted more…she was game.

Drawing in a deep breath, she clarified, "Would you like a cup of coffee, Coop?"

He nodded slowly. "Yes, I'd love a cup."

She poured his coffee and he walked over to take the cup from her hand. Their fingers brushed and her stomach curled with pleasure.

"Thanks," he said.

"You're welcome."

They both took a sip of their coffees. Despite trying not to love him, she wanted to get to know him. Like she'd told him earlier, she was very familiar with his parents' company. It was on the Fortune 500 list, which meant he came from money. He'd said the reason he'd wanted to become a SEAL was that the work was a better fit for his personality. And he'd become a SEAL with his parents' blessing. She knew things didn't always work that way for the sons of important families.

"It's late. I hadn't intended to impose on you by spending the night. I'll leave now if you want me to."

She looked at him over the rim of her cup. Did she want him to leave? No, she didn't. "There's no need, unless you want to go. You'll probably be back in the morning for breakfast anyway."

He chuckled. "Only if I get an invitation."

"You have an invitation, Coop. I told you, you can spend as much time with Laramie as you want."

He nodded and took a sip of his coffee. "In that case, I'd like to ask you something."

"What?" she asked.

"What plans do you and Laramie have for the holidays?"

She thought about his question. "Just a quiet time at home this year. It will be Laramie's first Christmas where he understands that the holidays are special. I've been telling him that if he's a good boy, Santa will bring him something nice. He's been keeping his toys put away and getting better with potty training." She paused before asking, "Why did you want to know about my plans for the holidays?"

"Because I'm hoping I can join the two of you." He drew in a deep breath. "And before you ask, the answer is no. I had no plans to spend Christmas with my folks."

Bristol remembered the last holiday they'd spent together. At that time, he'd given her the impression that he and his parents weren't close. Now was just as good a time as any to ask him about it. After all, his parents were her son's only living grandparents. In fact, the only living relatives Laramie had besides her and Coop, as far as she knew. If anything were to ever happen to her or Coop…

She suddenly needed to know about the people who might one day be responsible for her son. "You're welcome to join us, but I want you to tell me about your parents, Coop. Laramie's grandparents."

He leaned against her art table, avoiding her stacks of supplies. "What do you want to know?"

She shrugged. "Mainly, why you never want to spend the holidays with them?"

A part of Coop wanted to think her question was simple enough. But when it came to his parents, nothing was simple unless you accepted them for who they were. He'd done that a long time ago.

"Come on, let's sit on the sofa and I'll tell you about them."

"Okay."

Together, they sat down. To be on the safe side, since she was too desirable for her own good, he sat at the other end of the sofa. He took a sip of his coffee and said, "I think my parents are swell people who after nearly thirty-five years of marriage still love each other deeply."

He chuckled. "I wouldn't be wrong if I were to say they were obsessed with each other. I was told by both sets of my grandparents—who are deceased now—that it had been that way from the first, when they'd met at Harvard. Dad was from Laredo, Texas, and Mom from Laramie, Wyoming."

She lifted a brow. "Laramie?"

"Yes, and before you ask, the answer is yes. She named me after the city where she was born. She loved it that much and tried getting my father to move there after they were married. But he was a Texan through and through. He'd come from generations of ranchers, but he gave up that way of life, deciding not to follow in his father's, grandfather's and great-grandfather's footsteps as a rancher. He was the suit-and-tie kind. After college, he and my mom lived in Austin and started a business. Less than a year after graduating from college, the two of them were married. I was born three years later."

"No wonder your parents were so understanding about allowing you to have the career you wanted. They'd faced the same challenge."

"Yes, but my paternal grandparents weren't as understanding. They thought Dad was throwing away his legacy. Especially since my father was their only child."

He paused to take another sip of coffee. "I'm told that my mom's pregnancy with me was difficult. At one point, they thought she would die. My father was even told he might have to choose to either save his wife or his child. He picked his wife. But a top specialist arrived and assured my father he could save us both. He did. However, I think I was still a stark reminder to my dad of how close he came to losing Mom."

Bristol frowned, and he thought it was cute. "Surely,

he didn't hold you responsible and mistreat you in any way."

"No, not at all. Dad was good. However, my parents' relationship took a turn. They were always close, but I think nearly losing Mom freaked Dad out. After that he was determined to spend every moment he could with her…for the rest of their lives. They take more trips than I can count every year, and they have a tradition of spending the holidays together somewhere—usually with friends in England. Like I told you before, I've never spent the holidays with my parents. I've always spent them with my grandparents on their ranch. And trust me, I had no complaints. My grandparents were the greatest. I loved being out on their ranch."

"Did you ever feel resentful of your parents for not spending time with you?"

He knew it was hard to understand his relationship with his parents, but for her he wanted to try to explain. "It's not that my parents never spent time with me, Bristol, because they did. They were very active in my life while growing up and there were a number of trips we took together."

He took another sip of coffee. "Thanks to them, I saw most of the world before my sixteenth birthday. There was never a time I didn't think my parents loved me. However, I always knew they loved each other more."

"And you didn't have a problem with that?"

"No. I had friends whose parents didn't even like each other, couldn't stand to be in the same room together. Some of their parents divorced as soon as they finished school and my friends knew they had been the glue that held their parents' unhappy marriages together. That wasn't the case with my parents. There was never any doubt in my mind that Dad and Mom loved each other to the moon and back."

He didn't say anything for a minute, then he added, "When they thought I was dead, they went bonkers. I think they got even closer, if such a thing is possible with them. When I was found alive, they refused to let me out of their sight at first. They even questioned if I should continue being a SEAL. I knew they were worried, but I wasn't used to all the attention, at least not from them. I couldn't wait until I finished my recuperation period to return to work."

She spun her cup in her hands and asked, "What happened to your grandparents' ranch?"

"They willed it to me, although they were fully aware of my career as a SEAL. But my grandparents also knew I would manage the ranch as well as become a SEAL. For the ranch, I hired the right people to take care of it until I retire from the military, which will be in about six years. Some of the men working at the ranch for me used to work for my grandparents and can be trusted."

She nodded. "What kind of ranch is it?"

"It was always a cattle ranch but thanks to Bane's family, the Westmorelands, I've added horses. Several of his family members own a horse breeding and training company. They needed another holding depot before shipping the horses off to be trained. That's where my ranch comes in. So, I guess my ranch is a horse ranch, as well."

"Do you go there often?"

"Not as much as I would like. When I do go there

it's mainly to check on things. My men have everything pretty much under control."

"I'm glad."

A part of him believed she was, which made him say, "I want to show you and Laramie my ranch one day." He would tell her that much. He wouldn't tell her yet that he planned to make it his primary home for whenever Laramie visited.

She smiled and he felt a stirring in his stomach. "I'd love to see it, Coop. I know Laramie will, too. He loves horses."

"Then it's settled. I will take the two of you there after the holidays." Standing, he said, "I've kept you from your work long enough."

She smiled, standing, as well. "I'm okay. I was about to come to a stopping point anyway."

"You do this every night? Paint while Laramie sleeps?"

"Not every night. Just whenever the urge hits."

Funny, she should mention urges. At that moment, he was swamped with another urge. "Speaking of urges, Bristol," he said, setting his cup aside.

"What about them?"

"I feel one coming on myself."

She smiled. "You want to try your hand at painting?"

He chuckled. "No. It's not an urge to paint."

"Oh? What kind of urge is it?"

He leaned over and whispered in her ear. She smiled and placed her own coffee cup on the table. She moved closer and wrapped her arms around his neck. "In that case, I think we need to deal with these urges of yours."

"I agree." He swept her off her feet and headed toward her bedroom.

# Sixteen

Coop felt something poke him against his nose and he snatched his eyes open. He saw a miniature pair of eyes and a little hand right in his face. "You in my mommy's bed," his son all but accused.

Yes, he was in Laramie's mommy's bed. Before Coop could open his mouth to assure his son that everything was okay, Laramie had pulled himself up on the bed and crawled over him, saying, "Move over, Daddy." The little boy then planted himself in the middle of the bed, unceremoniously separating Coop and Bristol like the parting of the Red Sea.

"Laramie!" Bristol said, quickly sitting up after coming awake. "Be nice."

"He in your bed, Mommy."

Bristol yawned and ran a hand through her son's curls. "I know and it's okay. Good morning, Laramie."

He wrapped his arms around his mother's neck. "Good morning, Mommy."

Then, as if satisfied, Laramie slid beneath the covers and closed his eyes.

Bristol glanced over at Coop and smiled. "Sorry about that."

"Hey, don't apologize. I take it he does this every morning."

She nodded, pushing a mass of hair back from her face. "Yes. And as you can see it's not quite six o'clock. He comes in here, gets in my bed and will go back to sleep for another hour or so, then he'll wake up hungry. That's how we start our day."

For Coop that was a bummer because he'd planned to start his day by making love to her. Now, thanks to their son, those plans would be canned. But son or no son, Coop intended to get a good morning kiss. He leaned over and placed a kiss on her lips. "Good morning, Bristol."

She smiled. "Good morning, Coop."

He returned her smile. He'd liked waking up with her while in Paris and he liked waking up with her now. Even after making love to her multiple times last night, he still had a lot of sexual energy to work off and he knew only one other way to do so besides making love to Bristol.

"I'm going to the fitness center."

She lifted a brow. "The fitness center?"

"Yes, back at the hotel. I'm used to working out every morning." Usually he worked out twice a day. "I'll be back for breakfast if that's okay."

"That's fine. We'll be here."

"I'm counting on it." He leaned over and kissed

her again, this time a little longer, before easing out
of bed. He slid into his jeans and went into the con-
necting bathroom. When he returned a few moments
later, he saw she had drifted off to sleep with Laramie cuddled close.

As he finished dressing, he couldn't stop looking at
them. Something deep tugged at his heart. He wasn't
sure how to deal with all these emotions. For years,
he'd stayed in control of all relationships he was in-
volved in. Usually, none were for the long-term. He'd
been determined that no woman would ever rule his
heart.

He liked his freedom. Besides, his work as a SEAL
wasn't conducive to a normal family life. He didn't
know from one month to the next where a mission
might take him or for how long he'd be gone. He'd always enjoyed the adventure, the excitement, the quest
and, yes, even the danger. Definitely the danger. It was
enough to get your blood pumping and your adrenaline flowing.

But, he thought, studying Bristol while she slept,
she got his blood pumping and his adrenaline flowing, as well. And when he thought about what they'd
shared last night, he couldn't help but smile. Then his
smile widened and he knew why. He was happy. Truly
happy. And the two people responsible for his happiness were sleeping in that bed. In the last forty-eight
hours, his life had changed.

Already, he could admit he wouldn't want it any
other way.

When he finished dressing, he walked back over to
the bed to stare down at them. At her. He wondered
if she had any idea what she did to him, what she had

done to him three years ago. Resisting her hadn't been an option.

Bristol had gotten next to him without much effort and there hadn't been anything he could do about it.

Other than to fall in love with her.

That admission shook him to the core. He hadn't seen that coming. But now that he knew the truth, he had to accept it.

He loved her.

He drew in a deep breath. If he analyzed his behavior over the past three years, he probably would have realized he'd fallen in love with her the moment he and the guys had walked into that café in Paris. He'd seen her staring at him. He was certain he'd lost his heart then and there.

He'd left everyone at the table to approach her, determined to introduce himself before they could. Now his actions made sense. Love explained everything. Including the importance of those memories to his survival as well as why he'd returned to Paris looking for her as soon as he'd recuperated. When he'd accepted that she had been lost to him forever, he'd moved on. He'd been living a satisfied life but not a truly happy one.

There had to be a reason their paths had crossed in New York after all this time, a reason they had a child, who would always be a bond between them. And more than anything he also believed, whether she agreed or not, there was a purpose behind her decision to concoct a fake marriage and take his name.

He wanted Bristol and Laramie to always be a part of his life. He might not have planned for the recent turn of events, but now that he was faced with this little family of his, he had no regrets.

He was well aware that Bristol harbored reservations about making their marriage real, but he intended to get rid of whatever roadblocks stood in their way.

She didn't love him yet, but in the end she would. He was a determined man and when he came to a decision there was no stopping him.

He turned and walked out of her bedroom.

Bristol was in the middle of preparing breakfast when her phone rang. Was it Coop letting her know he wouldn't make it back for breakfast? Upon waking up again, Laramie had seemed a little disappointed that Coop had left. She had to admit, she was, too.

As she put the biscuits in the oven, she thought about how he'd found her in her studio working. He had been a distraction, but a welcome one. They had talked. But the one thing he hadn't said was whether or not he'd told his parents about Laramie. And about their fake marriage. If so, what did his parents think of all this?

When she grabbed the phone, she saw from the caller ID that it was Margie. "Yes, Margie?"

"Are you in a better mood today?"

Bristol raised a brow. "Was I in a bad mood yesterday?"

"I thought so. I might have upset you with those things I said about your husband. If I did, I'm sorry."

Bristol drew in a deep breath. Margie's words from yesterday had annoyed her. "There is a lot about my relationship with him that you don't know." And one of them was the fact he was not really her husband.

"Then enlighten me. Let's do lunch today."

Bristol nibbled on her bottom lip. Today was not a good day. She didn't like having to ask Ms. Charlotte to keep an eye on Laramie at the last minute. There might be a chance Coop would be available to watch him, but she couldn't depend on that. On top of those conflicts, she and Coop still had more to work through. They needed to decide how to move forward. He wanted to spend the holidays with them and she was fine with that. What she didn't want was what they'd shared last night muddying the waters.

She didn't want him to think that just because she'd allowed him in her bed she'd allow him into her life. That wasn't the case.

"Tomorrow will be better, Margie," she heard herself say.

"Okay, and tomorrow would it be a good time for you and Steven to talk?"

Margie's words got her attention. "Talk about what?"

Margie chuckled. "Honestly, Bristol, have you forgotten he represents a company who's a client? A client who made it possible for you to leave that boring job to stay home with your son and paint every day."

No, she hadn't forgotten, mainly because Margie refused to let her. She just didn't understand why Margie couldn't see that Bristol and Steven didn't click. "Fine, as long as this is strictly a business meeting, Margie."

"What other kind of meeting would I arrange? You don't like Steven, I get that now, although for Pete's sake, I don't know why. But it's your choice. Call me later and tell me when would be a good time to get together tomorrow."

"All right. I'll talk to you later."

As soon as she clicked off the phone and placed it aside, her doorbell rang. "Daddy's back, Mommy!"

The excitement in her son's voice touched her. At least he wasn't annoyed like he'd been this morning when he'd discovered his favorite spot in her bed already occupied. Once he'd gone to sleep and woken back up, he'd been team Coop all over again. "Yes, sweetheart, I think your daddy is back."

Putting the kitchen towel aside, she left the kitchen and headed toward the door.

"Good morning. I got you this," Coop said, handing her a huge poinsettia. There was a florist shop by the hotel and when he'd seen it this morning he knew he wanted to get it for her.

"Thanks. It's beautiful, Coop."

"You're welcome. I liked it when I saw it. It looks healthy and there are leaves that will be turning red in a few days."

She smiled. "Come on in." She stepped aside. "I just put the biscuits in the oven."

"Biscuits? You can make biscuits?"

"Yes, thanks to Aunt Dolly."

He entered, pulling off his Stetson and hanging his jacket on the coatrack. "I knew you could cook but claiming you can make biscuits has elevated you to another level."

She smiled. "That's good to know."

He watched as she placed the potted plant on a small table not far from the Christmas tree. It was hard to believe it was a week before Christmas, but in New York it was hard to forget the season. There seemed to be a Santa on every corner and all the light posts were decorated with wreaths.

"So, what do you think?" she asked, turning to stand beside the plant he'd given her.

His focus was on her when he said, "I wish I could have seen you pregnant."

"Where did that come from?" she asked, smiling.

"You asked what I thought and those were my thoughts while seeing you standing there, knowing my son is in the kitchen sitting at the table."

"Coloring."

He chuckled. "Yes, coloring."

She didn't say anything for a minute. "While pregnant, I looked like a blimp."

He crossed the floor to stop in front of her. He cupped her chin in his hand. "I bet you looked beautiful." He leaned down and brushed his lips across hers.

Then, as if she needed time to compose herself, she said, "The biscuits are about ready to come out the oven."

She hurried to the kitchen.


A couple hours later, Bristol stood in front of her easel. The sound of her son's laughter could be heard all the way upstairs, letting her know he was enjoying another day of Coop's company.

Her thoughts shifted back to breakfast. Laramie had been glad to see his father and had talked a mile a minute. Just like yesterday, after breakfast Coop had volunteered to help clean up the kitchen. Although she'd told him his help wasn't needed, he'd given it anyway. And she would inwardly admit there had been something comfortable about him helping with kitchen chores.

Her thoughts shifted to the poinsettia he'd given her. It was big and beautiful and looked like it belonged right in the spot she'd placed it. It had been so thoughtful of him to bring it for her, and it made her feel special, although she wished it didn't. The only other man who'd given her flowers had been her father. He had arrived at their first meeting with flowers and had given her flowers on her birthday ever since. Even after his death the flowers were delivered. They were always a beautiful bouquet and the card always said, "You are forever loved, Dad."

She wiped the tears from her eyes that always sprang up when she thought of her father and the little time they'd had together. But he was still making a positive impact on her life. The same way she believed Coop would make a positive impact on Laramie's life. He was spending time with their son and that meant a lot. Laramie would miss Coop when he left but he would look forward to his father's return.

If he returned…

She drew in a sharp breath as fear gripped her. She didn't want to think of the risk Coop took whenever he left on a covert operation, but she couldn't push it from her mind. Although he'd told her little about his work, he had explained to her in Paris that most of his missions were classified and couldn't be discussed. She wondered how families of navy SEALs dealt with not knowing from one day to the next the whereabouts of their loved ones and when they would return.

The sound of her cell phone snapped her out of her

reverie. She grabbed it off the table and smiled when she saw the caller was Dionne. "Hi, what's up?"

"Just calling to check on you. Are you and my godson okay?"

Bristol smiled. "We're fine. Just getting used to having a male presence around." She thought of how Coop had looked, standing on her doorstep that morning wearing a Stetson, jeans, suede jacket and boots. You could take the man out of Texas but you couldn't take Texas out of the man.

"A hot male presence, right?"

She thought about what had taken place in her bed last night and hot was just one adjective she could use. Other descriptions definitely came to mind but since Dionne had said hot... "Um, you can't imagine just how hot."

"*Oui!* Tell me!"

Bristol laughed. "No details for now. I need to prepare Laramie's lunch."

"Okay, but you will tell me later."

"Yes, later."

"You sound happy, Bristol."

Did she? "It's the holidays. Of course I sound happy."

"Usually you're not cheerful this time of year. Those memories of your aunt..."

Yes, there would always be memories of her aunt, who'd died over the holidays. "I know. At least I was here when it happened."

"Yes, I was there, too. I got to meet her. She was so nice."

"She was super."

They talked about other things while Dionne

brought Bristol up to date on her family and the other friends Bristol had left behind in Paris. "Bristol?"

"Yes?"

"Have you decided what you're going to do?"

Bristol frowned. "About what?"

"Your fake marriage. We went to a lot of trouble to make it seem real."

Bristol didn't say anything at first. She and Coop still hadn't decided how to proceed. "A fake divorce makes sense then, doesn't it? But then why waste money undoing something that wasn't real anyway?"

"Is that what he wants? To undo it?"

"I don't know what he wants. It only came up once. We need to talk about it again and make a decision," she said. "Everyone here thinks I was a widow and then out of the clear blue sky my husband reappears. It placed him in an awkward situation since he had no idea everyone thought we were married until I told him."

"Why not make it a real marriage under the pretense of renewing your vows?"

"Because there is no love between us."

Bristol knew what Dionne was going to say before she'd even said it. "There is love, Bristol, at least on your part. You loved him after Paris. Remember, I'm the one who told you he had died. I saw what that did to you and the grief you endured. You loved him too much. That much love doesn't just go away. There's no way you don't still love him."

Bristol opened her mouth to say that wasn't true, that she didn't still love Coop, but she couldn't lie to Dionne. "It doesn't matter. I intend to fall out of love with him."

"Why?"

Bristol drew in a deep breath. "You just said the reason. You saw the way I handled the news of his death and the grief I suffered as a result. I couldn't risk going through something like that a second time. I can't and I won't."

# Seventeen

For the second night in a row Coop stood aside while Bristol tucked their son into bed. Today had been a full day of activities. After breakfast he'd stretched out on the floor and helped Laramie put Lego blocks together. Then after lunch he had bundled his son up in his boots and coat and they'd walked to the park.

Bristol had invited Coop to stay for dinner and now he couldn't help wondering if she would invite him to stay the night. She really hadn't invited him last night, but their need for each other had pretty much made the decision for them.

There was a strong possibility she might send him packing after they had the little talk he intended for them to have. It was time he forced her hand on a few things.

"Laramie wants to tell you good-night."

Bristol's words broke into Coop's thoughts and he moved from leaning in the doorway to where his son lay, barely able to keep his eyes open. His son, who had captured his heart the moment he'd heard he existed.

"Daddy, you stay. Sleep in Mommy's bed, okay?"

He couldn't help but smile. His son was giving him permission even though Bristol hadn't done so. Instead of agreeing with Laramie, Coop said, "Good night, Laramie."

"Stay, Daddy. Sleep in Mommy's bed. Okay?"

Evidently Laramie wasn't going to let him off that easy. Was this the same kid who'd pushed his nose in this morning when he discovered Coop was in Bristol's bed? The same little fellow who'd crawled over him to claim his spot beside his mother?

"He will stay, Laramie. Now you need to go to sleep."

He glanced over at Bristol. Was that her way of giving him an invitation? But then all she'd assured their son was that he would stay, not necessarily that he would stay in her bed. Did that mean she planned to make him sleep on the sofa?

He'd tried deciphering her mood today. Although she'd been friendly enough, it had seemed as if she had a lot on her mind. That was fine. He had a lot on his, too. But still, he couldn't help wondering if she regretted the intimacy they'd shared last night. She hadn't mentioned it and neither had he.

"Love you, Mommy."

"Love you back, Laramie. See you in the morning." And just like the night before, Bristol leaned over and kissed him on the cheek. However, unlike last night, before drifting off to sleep Laramie said, "Love you, Daddy."

Coop felt a tug at his heart and a tightness in his throat. It boggled his mind how a child could love so easily. "I love you back, Laramie."

He and Bristol watched as their son drifted off to sleep.

When they left Laramie's room, Coop told her they needed to talk.

Did he regret sleeping with her last night? The morning had started off well…at least she'd thought so, when he'd returned and surprised her with that beautiful plant. However, since then he'd seemed quiet. More than once she'd noticed him studying her like she was a puzzle he was trying to put together. Why?

She looked across the room at him. He was staring at the Christmas tree. What was he thinking? She'd invited him to spend Christmas with her and Laramie. Then what? When would he be leaving New York for his next mission?

"Ready to talk?"

She wondered why he was asking her when he was the one who initiated the meeting. "I'm ready if you are."

He nodded and sat in the chair across from her. He looked at her for a few moments then he said, "I spoke with my attorney today."

"Oh? Why did you feel the need to do that?"

He leaned back in the chair and the fabric of his jeans emphasized his masculine thighs. She wished she didn't notice such things, but she did.

"Laramie is my heir and I wanted to include him in all my important documents."

"I see."

"I also needed legal advice on my rights as his father."

Bristol raised a brow. "Your rights?"

"Yes."

She frowned. "I don't understand. I thought I made it clear that I would never deny you access to Laramie and you could spend as much time with him as you want."

"Yes, but what if you decide to marry one day and your husband feels differently?"

"I don't ever plan to marry, so you have nothing to worry about."

"You don't know that."

"I don't know what?"

"That you never plan to marry. Things happen. You might change your mind."

Her frown deepened. "That won't happen."

"You can't be sure," he countered.

"Yes, I can."

He shook his head. "No, you can't. And because you can't, my attorney suggested that I take steps to protect my rights as Laramie's father by filing for joint custody."

Coop watched her lean forward in her seat, at full attention. Her eyes widened. "Joint custody?"

"Yes."

"That's crazy. You're not in this country most of the time. How can you even think about joint custody?"

"How can I not think about it, Bristol? In a way, it will make things easier on you."

"How do you figure that?" she asked, glaring at him.

"You will know what times during the year he will be with me and when he will be with you. One thing I'd like is to swap holidays every year."

"Swap holidays?" She asked the question like what he was requesting was the craziest thing she'd ever heard.

"Yes. I told you about the ranch I inherited from my grandparents. I want him to spend the holidays with me there next year. That will free you up to do whatever you want to do."

"Free me up? To do. Whatever I want. To do?"

She had enunciated each phrase. He could tell from the sound of her voice that her anger was increasing. "Yes. I figure with me pitching in, you'll be able to paint more. While I'm away as a SEAL, I plan on hiring a full-time nanny who—"

"A full-time nanny? You've got to be kidding." She inhaled and exhaled a few times and he knew she was trying to get her anger under control. "What's going on, Coop? What are you trying to do?"

He had no problem giving her an answer. "I'm trying to give you a reason to make our marriage real."

Bristol's pulse jumped a few notches as she inhaled deeply. "Why?" she asked him. "Why should we make our marriage real?"

He shifted again in his seat and she wondered if he'd done it on purpose to distract her. Did he have any idea how his movements always increased her hormone level?

"The foremost reason is our son. I just cited complications that could arise if we aren't married. Knowing I have a child is a game changer for me. It was never my intent to father a child until later in life, and like I told you, I don't regret him, Bristol. I appreciate everything you went through to bring him into this world. And just so you know, if the situation had been different and I hadn't been held hostage, if I had gotten your letter, you would not have been alone. I would have come to you. I would have been there for you and for my child."

"But how would you have been there, Coop? You're a part of the military's special services. When you leave on one of your missions you have no idea when you'll get back."

"True, but I would have taken the time off. The entire nine months if I had to. I would have made sure I was there for you. You would not have gone through your pregnancy alone."

He didn't say anything for a few moments. "I believe in accepting my responsibilities, Bristol, but, just so you know, I would not have asked you to marry me just because you were having a baby. I would have done right by my child and by you, but I would not have suggested marriage between us unless I thought it would work."

At least he was honest, she thought. "So given that, why do you think it will work now? We don't even know each other."

"We know enough and over the past couple of days we've found out more. We could be together for years and not know everything. Besides, I enjoy getting to know you."

He shifted again and her gaze followed the movement. "I know you are a good mother. As far as I'm concerned, you're the best. I can't think of anyone else I'd want to be the mother of my child. I watch you with Laramie and I know how much you love him and will always put him first. A part of me wants to envy that closeness, but I can't. I want to be a part of it, Bristol. You've given Laramie something special. A home."

His words reminded her of something her father had said. Even though her mother had robbed him of time with Bristol, in the end, he couldn't resent her mother when his heart was filled with gratitude to her for shaping Bristol into the woman she was. One who was loyal and independent. Not spoiled or selfish. Although her father had never said so, she knew he'd compared her to his other two kids. After living in their household for almost two years, she could plainly see that his wife's parenting skills had been vastly different from her mother's. Krista Lockett hadn't known how to tell her sons no.

"To me marriage is more than a piece of paper," he said, interrupting her thoughts. "I can't help but believe that, especially when I see my parents together and how they interact with each other. Even if there wasn't all that love, I believe there would still be trust, respect and friendship between them."

Unfortunately, Bristol thought, she'd never witnessed any such thing between a married couple. It had always been just her and her mother, and her mother had rarely dated. The few times she had, Bristol hadn't been introduced to the men. When she'd asked her mother about it, all she'd said was that until she met someone special, there was no reason to introduce her dates to her daughter. Evidently her mother never met anyone special. And as for her father's marriage to Krista, Bristol could honestly say she'd never felt any love in their relationship. They'd shared the same bedroom but that was about all. They'd lived separate lives.

Bristol drew in a deep breath as she thought about what Coop had said. Yes, there was trust and respect between them. She'd trusted him enough three years ago to invite him into her home and she still trusted him. She also respected him. In just two days he had made an impact on his son's life. And there was his love for his country and his willingness to put his life on the line to protect it. There was no doubt in her mind they could be friends as they got to know each other. Sex between them was good.

But what about the love?

That was something he hadn't mentioned. He didn't love her, whereas she'd loved him almost from the start. A part of her truly believed she'd fallen in love with him the moment she'd seen him in Paris. There was no way she would have agreed to an affair if she hadn't loved him.

But none of those feelings mattered because all the love, respect, trust and friendship in the world couldn't erase how she'd felt when she'd thought he'd died. That was a period in her life she couldn't relive. Somehow, she needed to make him understand that.

"What you said might be true, but there's a reason I can't marry you, Coop, and it's one I can't get beyond."

He lifted a brow. "And what reason is that?"

She met his gaze, held it and said, "You might die."

# Eighteen

"You might die…"

Coop stared at her, recalling their conversation last night when she'd said the same thing. Why was she so hung up on the possibility of him dying?

Something else he recalled her saying last night was that three years ago she'd thought he'd died like the others. At the time, he'd wondered what others she was talking about. Now he had an idea who they were. Her mother, father and aunt. All the people she'd ever cared about and loved.

His heart pounded hard in his chest. Did that mean she cared deeply for him, that she loved him?

What if he was right? The thought that she could love him as much as he loved her was more than he could have hoped for. There was only one way to find out.

"I vividly remember having this conversation with

you last night. Why are you so obsessed with the possibility of me dying, Bristol? Why are you so convinced I won't come back to you and Laramie?"

He watched her closely, saw how she went still, saw the stark look of fear come into her eyes. Their gazes locked for a minute longer and then she rubbed her hand down her face before meeting his eyes again. Then he saw the tears she was fighting to hold back.

"Talk to me, Bristol. Tell me," he said softly.

Bristol's mind shifted to that day when Dionne had arrived at her apartment and told her what she'd found out about Coop. How could she make him understand how she'd felt and why there was no way they could have a real marriage?

There was no way she could go through something like that again.

"When I thought you had died," she said, trying not to choke on the words, "I thought I was going to die, as well. It came as such a shock. I experienced pain like I'd never felt before. It was deeper than when I lost my mom, my dad and Aunt Dolly. And I felt so alone."

She fought back her tears to continue. "Then I suddenly felt my baby…our baby…move for the first time. It was like he was trying to reassure me that things would be all right. But the thought that I'd lost you was more than I could bear. Even when I told myself that I never had you, that all we'd had was a holiday affair and that I probably would not have seen you again anyway, it didn't matter. The thought of you dying like the others nearly destroyed me. It was only when I finally came to grips with the fact that I was having a baby…your baby…a baby that would always be a part of you, that I was able to move on with my life."

Coop stood and walked over to her, extending his hand out to her. She took it and he gently tugged her off the sofa and into his arms. It was only then that she realized she hadn't been able to hold back all her tears. A few were streaming down her face. How awful it was for him to see her like this, crying over a man who'd meant more to her than she'd meant to him. But when he tightened his arms around her, pulling her deeper into the warmth of his embrace, it didn't seem to matter.

"Knowing you cared that much means a lot to me, Bristol. Like I told you, you were never far from my thoughts when I was captured. Thoughts of you are what helped me survive."

"Why?" she asked, wanting to know why he'd thought of her.

"Because during those three days we were together, you made a lasting impression on me."

Like he'd made on her, she thought. However, he'd gone a step further in making her fall in love with him.

He pulled back and looked at her, forcing her to meet his gaze. "And as you can see, I am very much alive. No matter how much torture they inflicted on me, I refused to let those bastards break me—because of you."

She lifted a brow. "Because of me?"

"Yes. I convinced myself that I had to survive for you. That once I was rescued I had to get back to you."

Too bad he hadn't meant that, she thought.

"By the time I made it to Paris, you had left."

Bristol went still as she stared at him. "What did you say?" She was convinced she'd heard him wrong.

"After getting rescued I had to comply with military procedures and get both physical and psychiatric evaluations. That took about three months. Then I flew to Paris to see you. Your landlord said you'd moved back to the States and hadn't left a forwarding address."

Bristol's head began spinning. "You went to Paris looking for me?"

"Yes."

"But why?"

He gently cupped her chin in his hand. "I had to see you again and let you know those three days with you meant everything to me."

"They did?"

"Yes, and I just didn't know the depth of what they meant until I saw you again the other night. But it really hit me this morning when I saw you and Laramie in bed, sleeping. Then I knew for certain."

"What did you know?"

He dropped his hands from her face to wrap them around her waist. "That I had fallen in love with you."

His words made her head spin even more. "What did you just say?"

He smiled down at her. "I said I fell in love with you, during that time in Paris. I tried to convince myself it was about the sex, and maybe it was at first. But by the time I left your place I felt an attachment to you I've never felt to any other woman." A smile touched his lips. "Who knows? Maybe my body knew I'd left something behind with you that I've never left with another woman, my baby."

"Oh, Coop," she said, feeling more tears well in her eyes. "I love you, too, but I'm so afraid I might lose you again."

He pulled her into his arms and tightened his hold on her. "Shh, sweetheart, it's okay. In life there are no guarantees, we know that. That's why it's important to enjoy our time together. If nothing else, being close to death so many times has taught me not to sweat the small stuff and to appreciate life. Living it to the fullest is what I want to do with you and our son. Please don't deny me that."

He paused before adding, "You gave me the hope and the will to live before, which was how I survived that hellhole. And you will continue to give me hope whenever I go out on any covert operation, Bristol. Now I have two people to come back to. Both you and Laramie. The two people I love the most."

His words meant everything. They were what she'd needed to hear. But could she get past the thought of losing him again?

She tightened her arms around him knowing she had to get beyond those fears. For her sake, for his sake and for their son's. She had to be strong and believe there was a reason their lives had reunited after all this time.

She pulled back and went on tiptoe to place her lips to his. The moment their lips touched, intense heat consumed her. She felt it spreading to him. He tightened his hold on her.

His masculine scent invaded her nostrils as he took her mouth with an urgency that made her weak in the knees. When she shifted she felt the hardness of his erection pressing against the juncture of her thighs.

Bristol released pleasured moans with every stroke of his tongue. She needed this. She had to think positively and believe they'd been reunited for a reason. For a purpose. They would do what her parents didn't do and raise their child together.

He deepened the kiss and she felt it all the way to the bone.

Suddenly, he pulled back and looked deep into her eyes. "I need more."

She needed more, too. "Then take more. Give me more."

Nothing else needed to be said. He swept her off her feet and into his arms and carried her up the stairs.


"I love you, sweetheart," Coop said, after making love to Bristol again.

He pulled her into his arms and glanced over at the clock. They'd made love three times since coming upstairs and had gotten little sleep in between. If the other morning was anything to go by, he figured his son would be invading this room in a couple hours, and Coop and Bristol still needed to talk.

Coop knew she was about to drift off to sleep and he needed to get her attention. "Bristol?"

"Um?"

"Will you marry me?"

She didn't say anything at first, then she looked up at him. "I can't let fear have power over me, right?"

He nodded. "Right."

A smile touched the corners of her lips. "Then yes, Coop. I will marry you."

A huge smile touched his features. "How soon?"

She chuckled. "Can we get through the holidays first?"

He shrugged. "I guess we can."

She kissed him on the cheek. "Thanks for being so accommodating." Then she asked, "When do you have to leave for another mission?"

"End of January, and I want us married before I leave."

"That shouldn't be a problem," she said.

"As far as anyone knows, we are renewing our vows. There will only be a few who know the truth."

"Your teammates?"

"Yes, and my parents. I told them I loved you and if nothing else, they understand the love between two people and how strong it can be. They can't wait to meet you and Laramie."

She eyed him skeptically. "You sure about that?"

"I'm positive." And he was. Once the initial shock wore off, his parents had called him back. They were excited and happy to have a grandchild. Coop figured they must have decided Bristol couldn't be all bad since she hadn't shown up trying to claim any of his inheritance on behalf of her child after she'd gotten word he was dead.

"And since we won't have time for a real honeymoon until later, I thought it would be nice if I took you and Laramie to my ranch for a week or two before I head out. We can hire an interior decorator to spruce the place up while I'm gone."

"I'd love that. Would you prefer living there more so than here?" she asked him.

"Wherever you want to live is fine with me. We can even do both if you like."

"Yes, that might be best. But for some reason I think I'm going to like your ranch."

He hoped she did. He wanted Laramie to love Cooper's Bend as much as he had while growing up.

"You will check out of the hotel and move in here with us, right?"

He chuckled. "Yes, I'll move in here with you and Laramie and we will spend the holidays together."

"Good."

He pulled her closer. She was right, all was good, and as long as he had her in his life, everything would continue to be good.

Everything would be perfect.

# Epilogue

"I now pronounce you husband and wife. Laramie Cooper, you may kiss your bride."

Coop pulled Bristol into his arms and all he could think about was that she was now truly his. Legally so. When he felt a pull on his pants he broke off the kiss to glance down at his son.

"I want to kiss Mommy, too, Daddy."

Everyone laughed when Coop lifted his son up to kiss Bristol, as well.

He then glanced around. It had been a small wedding at the church Bristol attended. All his teammates had arrived yesterday with their wives, including Bane and Crystal. Coop's parents had gushed all over their grandson and Laramie enjoyed being the center of their attention.

Ms. Charlotte and her four sons attended and Coop

was glad to meet them. Bristol hadn't told him that all four worked for the New York Police Department. They assured Coop that whenever he was gone they would keep an eye on Bristol. It wouldn't be a problem since she lived next door to their mother and they routinely checked on her anyway.

Coop's mother had walked into Bristol's home that morning and her gaze had immediately latched on to the huge painting over her fireplace. When she asked Bristol about it, Bristol confessed it was a painting she and her father had done together. It was then that she'd told his mother who her father was. Coop thought he was going to have to pick his mother up off the floor. His very sophisticated mother had gotten giddy at the thought that her future daughter-in-law was the daughter of the famous artist, Randall Lockett.

The reception would be held in the church's dining hall, and tomorrow the three of them would fly to his ranch in Laredo. He couldn't wait to introduce his wife and son to ranch life at Cooper's Bend.

They would take a honeymoon when he got back from his next mission. Ms. Charlotte had agreed to watch Laramie for a week while they went to Jamaica.

"Ready to go to the reception Ms. Charlotte set up for us?" Bristol asked him.

Holding their son in his arms, Coop smiled at her. "Yes, sweetheart, I am ready. When it comes to you, I will always be ready."

"Thanks for inviting me, Bristol."

She smiled up at Colin Kusac. They had exchanged phone numbers that night at the gallery when she'd reunited with Coop. When Mr. Kusac had called to check up on her a few days later, she'd learned that just as she'd suspected, he was the person carrying out her father's wishes to make sure she got flowers every year on her birthday. He had explained that Randall had asked that of him before he'd died and Mr. Kusac had promised he would do so.

He'd also told her that he'd promised her father he would check on her from time to time. He confided that he knew how she'd been while living in Paris; and that when she returned to the United States to have her baby, he'd known about that, as well. He'd seen that night at the gallery as an opportunity to talk to her himself. She had discovered that Mr. Kusac—Colin—was one of the wealthiest men in New York and had come from old money.

"Thanks for standing in for Dad and giving me away."

"Thanks for asking me. I was honored to do so. Randall would have been proud of you today."

"Thank you."

They talked for a while longer and then the wives of Coop's teammates came up to say hello. She liked all the wives—Crystal, who was married to Bane, Layla, who was married to Viper, and Teri, who had been married to Mac from the start. They assured Bristol that she wasn't the only one with fears—that was part of being a SEAL wife. They would be part of her support team and would be there whenever she needed them. They even invited her to visit them at their homes. Everyone was excited when Viper and Layla announced they would be having a baby come early summer. They exchanged numbers with her and she knew they were women she would get to know as friends.

No sooner had the women walked off than Margie appeared, all smiles. Bristol knew why.

"I can't believe your husband is connected to so much wealth. Who would have thought his parents would be *those* Coopers. And that he's their heir."

"Yes, who would have thought?" Bristol smiled, knowing how Margie's mind worked.

"You did good, choosing him over Steven."

Bristol decided not to say that Steven hadn't even been in the running. When Margie left, Coop appeared at Bristol's side. "A car will be picking us up in a few minutes for the airport."

His parents' jet would fly them to Texas, where they would stay for a week on a short vacation with Laramie. After Coop had told Laramie about the horses, their son had been bubbling over with excitement to visit the ranch.

Not caring that they had an audience, Coop pulled his wife into his arms and whispered, "I love you."

She smiled up at him. "And I love you, too."

And she meant that from the bottom of her heart.

\* \* \* \* \*

*A WIFE FOR A WESTMORELAND*
*THE PROPOSAL*

*FEELING THE HEAT*
*TEXAS WILD*
*ONE WINTER'S NIGHT*
*ZANE*
*CANYON*
*STERN*
*THE REAL THING*
*THE SECRET AFFAIR*
*BREAKING BAILEY'S RULES*
*BANE*

*And don't miss the first*
*Westmoreland Legacy novel, Viper's story*

*THE RANCHER RETURNS*

*If you're on Twitter, tell us what you think of*
*Harlequin Desire! #harlequindesire*

# COMING NEXT MONTH FROM

### Available January 2, 2018

## #2563 THE RANCHER'S BABY
*Texas Cattleman's Club: The Impostor* • by Maisey Yates
When Selena Jacobs's ex-husband shows up at his own funeral, it's her estranged best friend who insists on staying with her to keep her safe. But living with the one who got away gets complicated when one night leads to an unexpected surprise...

## #2564 TAMING THE TEXAN
*Billionaires and Babies* • by Jules Bennett
Former military man turned cowboy Hayes Elliott is back at the family ranch to recover from his injuries. The last thing he needs is to fall into bed with temptation...especially when she's a sexy single mom who used to be married to his best friend!

## #2565 LITTLE SECRETS: UNEXPECTEDLY PREGNANT
by Joss Wood
Three years ago, Sage pushed Tyce away. Three months ago, they shared one (mistaken) red-hot night of passion. Now? She's pregnant and can't stay away from the man who drives her wild. But as passion turns to love, secrets and fears could threaten everything...

## #2566 CLAIMING HIS SECRET HEIR
*The McNeill Magnates* • by Joanne Rock
Damon McNeill's wife has returned a year after leaving him—but between her amnesia and the baby boy she's cradling, he's suddenly unsure of what really happened. Will he untangle the deception and lies surrounding her disappearance in time to salvage their marriage?

## #2567 CONTRACT BRIDE
*In Name Only* • by Kat Cantrell
CEO Warren Garinger knows better than to act on his fantasies about his gorgeous employee Tilda Barrett, but when she needs a green card marriage, he volunteers to say, "I do." Once he's her husband, though, keeping his distance is no longer an option!

## #2568 PREGNANT BY THE CEO
*The Jameson Heirs* • by HelenKay Dimon
Derrick Jameson dedicated his life to the family business, and all he needs to close the deal is the perfect fiancée. When the sister of his nemesis shows up, desperate to make amends, it's perfect...until a surprise pregnancy brings everyone's secrets to light!

HDCNM1217

# Get 2 Free Books,

## Plus 2 Free Gifts—

### just for trying the Reader Service!

HARLEQUIN *Desire*

She wandered out of the kitchen and into the living room just
as the door to the guest bedroom opened and Knox walked out,
pulling his T-shirt over his head—but not quickly enough. She
caught a flash of muscled, tanned skin and…

She was completely immobilized by the sight of her best
friend's muscles.

It wasn't like she had never seen Knox shirtless before.
But it had been a long time. And the last time, he had most
definitely been married.

Not that she had forgotten he was hot when he was married
to Cassandra. It was just that…he had been a married man. And
that meant something to Selena. Because it meant something
to him.

It had been a barrier, an insurmountable one, even bigger
than that whole long-term friendship thing. And now it wasn't
there. It just wasn't. He was walking out of the guest bedroom
looking sleep rumpled and entirely too lickable. And there was

just…nothing stopping them from doing what men and women did.

She'd had a million excuses for not doing that. For a long time. She didn't want to risk entanglements, didn't want to compromise her focus. Didn't want to risk pregnancy. Didn't have time for a relationship.

But she was in a place where those things were less of a concern. This house was symbolic of that change in her life. She was making a home. And making a home made her want to fill it. With art, with warmth, with knickknacks that spoke to her.

With people.

She wondered, then. What it would be like to actually live with a man? To have one in her life? In her home? In her bed?

And just like that she was fantasizing about Knox in her bed…

*Don't miss*
THE RANCHER'S BABY
*by* New York Times *bestselling author Maisey Yates,*
*the first book in the* **TEXAS CATTLEMAN'S CLUB:**
**THE IMPOSTOR** *series! Available January 2018*
*wherever Harlequin® Desire books and ebooks are sold.*

*And then follow the whole saga—*
*Will the scandal of the century lead to love for these rich ranchers?*
*The Rancher's Baby by* New York Times *bestselling author Maisey Yates*
*Rich Rancher's Redemption by* USA TODAY *bestselling author Maureen Child*
*A Convenient Texas Wedding by Sheri WhiteFeather*
*Expecting a Scandal by Joanne Rock*
*Reunited…with Baby by* USA TODAY *bestselling author Sara Orwig*
*The Nanny Proposal by Joss Wood*
*Secret Twins for the Texan by Karen Booth*
*Lone Star Secrets by Cat Schield*

www.Harlequin.com

# *LOVE*
# Harlequin
# romance?

Join our Harlequin community to share your thoughts and connect with other romance readers!

Be the first to find out about promotions, news, and exclusive content!

Sign up for the Harlequin e-newsletter and download a free book from any series at

**www.TryHarlequin.com**

---

**CONNECT WITH US AT:**

Harlequin.com/Community

 Facebook.com/HarlequinBooks

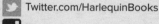 Twitter.com/HarlequinBooks

 Instagram.com/HarlequinBooks

Pinterest.com/HarlequinBooks

ReaderService.com

**ROMANCE WHEN
YOU NEED IT**

HSOCIAL2017

Want to give in to temptation with
steamy tales of irresistible desire?

Check out **Harlequin® Presents®**,
**Harlequin® Desire** and
**Harlequin® Kimani™ Romance** books!

**New books available every month!**

---

**CONNECT WITH US AT:**

Harlequin.com/Community

Facebook.com/HarlequinBooks

Twitter.com/HarlequinBooks

Instagram.com/HarlequinBooks

Pinterest.com/HarlequinBooks

ReaderService.com

**ROMANCE WHEN
YOU NEED IT**

PGENRE2017

# THE WORLD IS BETTER WITH

## *Romance*

Harlequin has everything from contemporary, passionate and heartwarming to suspenseful and inspirational stories.

Whatever your mood, we have a romance just for you!